DEEP WATERS

A RICK WATERS NOVEL

CARIBBEAN ADVENTURE SERIES
BOOK EIGHT

ERIC CHANCE STONE

LOST AND FOUND PUBLISHING

ACKNOWLEDGMENTS

I would like to thank my beta readers Bavette Battern, Mike Keevil, Carroll Scadden Shroyer, Kathy Pompeo.

Special thanks to my proofreader Carroll Scadden Shroyer, who also did the editing on this one.

Thanks to my second proofreader Teri

Also special thanks to Jamie Cryer for always being supportive and sending me book ideas from time to time. He's a good friend.

I'd like to thank Kim-Cara Lalonde for putting up with me during all the hours I sit in front of my computer writing. And also making me go outside every once and while, see the sun and exercise.

Very special thanks to all the wonderful readers who have supported me on this journey and bought my pre-orders, signed up for my newsletter and continued to support me. Without you, I couldn't do this. As long as y'all keep reading, I'll keep writing.

Lastly, many thanks to my writing mentor Wayne Stinnett, for always being just a phone call away when I have a question.

ABOUT THE AUTHOR

Eric Chance Stone was born and raised on the gulf coast of Southeast Texas. An avid surfer, sailor, scuba diver, fisherman and treasure hunter, Eric met many bigger than life characters on his adventures across the globe. Wanting to travel after college, he got a job with Northwest Airlines and moved to Florida. Shortly thereafter transferred to Hawaii, then Nashville. After years of being a staff songwriter in Nashville, he released his first album, Songs For Sail in 1999, a tropically inspired collection of songs. He continued to write songs and tour and eventually landed a gig with Sail America and Show Management to perform at all international boat shows where his list of characters continued to grow.

He moved to the Virgin Islands in 2007 and became the official entertainer for Pusser's Marina Cay in the BVI. After several years in the Caribbean, his fate for telling stories was sealed.

Upon release of his 15th CD, All The Rest, he was inspired to become a novelist after a chance meeting with Wayne

Stinnett. Wayne along with Cap Daniels, Chip Bell and a few others, became his mentors and they are all good friends now. Eric currently resides in Destin, Florida with his fiancée Kim-Cara and their three exotic birds, Harley, Marley and Ozzy.

Inspired by the likes of Clive Cussler's Dirk Pitt, Wayne Stinnett's Jesse McDermitt, Cap Daniels Chase Fulton, Chip Bell's Jake Sullivan and many more, Eric's tales are sprinkled with Voodoo, Hoodoo and kinds of weird stuff. From the bayous of Texas to the Voodoo dens of Haiti, his twist of reality will take you for a ride. His main character Rick Waters is a down to earth good ol' boy, adventurist turned private eye, who uses his treasure hunting skills and street smarts to solve mysteries.

Follow Eric Chance Stone -
    Website: http://www.EricChanceStone.com
    Facebook: https://www.facebook.com/RickWatersSeries

CHAPTER 1

Rick and Jules stood motionless at the entrance of their condo in Destin. They just stared silently at two large wooden crates, emblazoned on the sides with the words "Helga One" and "Helga Two," sitting ominously in the center of their living room.

They were weary from their adventurous return journey from Africa as they stepped into their newly remodeled Destin condo. Rick took three steps towards the crates and pulled a manila envelope from a clear plastic invoice holder fastened to one of the boxes. He read it aloud.

Dear Rick and Jules,

I hope this letter finds you both in good health and high spirits. As I sit here reflecting on our recent adventures in Africa, I am filled with an overwhelming sense of gratitude for the unwavering support and dedication you have shown throughout our time together. Your help was essential in Africa and as token of appreciation from myself and Interpol, please enjoy "Helga One" and "Helga Two." The gift that keeps giving. LOL

With kindest regards,

Renato

"Well, I'll be damned! He took me seriously when I said I wanted one of those Helga's," said Rick.

The Helga's Rick was referring to, were two identical water massage machines Rick fell in love with, while in Africa on a case. He had mentioned to Renato, the senior agent from Interpol, how much he enjoyed the massage and wished he had one, but never dreamed he would actually send him one, let alone, two.

They were both too tired to even begin to unbox the massive water massage machines, plus they weren't sure where they'd best fit in their condo. Jules suggested the balcony; one against each side wall. Rick decided he'd need to measure and make sure they'd fit. But first it was time for some *ha-ha, clink-clink.* A phrase Rick often used to describe having laughs and drinks.

Jules told Rick to go ahead and sit down on the balcony and she put a snack tray together for them and brought out the wine she had picked up at Publix on the ride back from the airport. Rick had stayed in the Uber while she went inside.

Once on the balcony, he kicked off his shoes and took in a deep slow breath of the salt laden Destin beach air. It was a smell he had missed. Jules sat down with a tray of charcu-terie she quickly put together along with the bottle of red wine, but just one wine glass. She sat a cold bottle of Perrier on the table by her chair. Rick gave her a strange confused look.

"Not in the mood for wine?" he asked.

"Yeah, I am, but remember the night we spent in Africa at the reserve?"

"How could I forget? It was a perfect night. We stayed up late after watching the sun set over the African plains and I held you on the screened-in porch as we swayed to the sound of the wind in the reeds. We made love to the back-drop of the mighty Zambezi River. It's my favorite memory of Africa. Why?"

Jules eagerly approached Rick with a mixture of excite-ment and apprehension, holding in her trembling hand a positive pregnancy test kit. With a radiant smile on her face, she revealed the life-altering news that they were going to be parents. Rick's eyes widened in disbelief and joy as he real-ized the magnitude of this moment. Overwhelmed by emotions, they embraced tightly, their hearts filled with a profound sense of love and anticipation for the new chapter that awaited them. Rick was beaming.

"I'm so happy Jules. How long have you known?"

"Not long. Actually, when we stopped at Publix, I bought the test. I'm about two weeks late and I had a pretty good idea. I just wanted to be sure before I told you," she said.

Rick jumped up and gave her a huge hug and kissed her neck gently.

"Don't open the wine. I tell you what. Since you can't drink. I'll support you and I won't drink. How's that sound?"

"You don't have to do that Rick."

"I know, I know but my liver could use a break. We'll both be healthier for it."

"That's so sweet of you baby," replied Jules.

Rick jogged to the kitchen and grabbed a bottle of Perrier and another wine glass, filled them both up and held it up towards Jules.

Click clink!

"Cheers. Here's to our first bambino, be it a boy or a girl," said Rick.

Jules blushed and took a swallow of her Perrier as did Rick. After a nice light dinner, they crawled into their own bed. It had been a long time since they'd slept at home. They held each other and dozed off rather quickly. Rick awakened before sunrise and made coffee. He wanted to pamper Jules and let her sleep. He checked in on her after the coffee was done and she was still in dream land, so he quietly stepped outside and went down to their office on the first floor. It had been months since he had been inside and was sure there was a pile of mail to deal with. He was pleasantly surprised to see no mail and a note on his iMac from his partner Gary Haas.

Hey bud. Took the jet to Destin the day you and Jules left

Africa and took care of all the mail and messages we had. We were offered a couple of cases and we can discuss when y'all get here. The new ship captain Larry Lane seems to be working out fine. I can't wait for ya'll to see this ship. She's a beauty!

Gary

P.S. What the hell is a Helga One & Two?

Rick laughed aloud and crumpled the note and threw it in the waste basket. The office smelled clean and fresh. Gary was always thinking of others before himself. It amazed Rick how selfless he was. A few years back before Gary won the huge lotto, he would have given the shirt off of his own back to help someone and after winning, that didn't change. Except the shirts were no longer Walmart specials. Gary now dressed to impress but the money hadn't really changed him. In fact, it made him even more generous. It made Rick think about all the kind things Gary had done since his big win, like the time he bought the entire crew brand new Ford Badlands Broncos in each person's favorite color, just because he felt bad that some of Rick's crew were sharing rides. Then there was the time he used his own private jet to fly Johnie, Rick's first mate, and Possum, Rick's best friend on a joy ride on his new jet, just for fun. Not to mention the time they needed to rent a motorhome for a case in Mississippi and instead of renting, Gary bought a Prevost Tour bus. He had bought both towers where they all were given condos and he paid for all the renovations. He was a very giving person. Then there was the ship.

Rick had made an offhand comment about how cool it would be to have a treasure hunting ship instead of using Nine-Tenths, Rick's charter boat for treasure hunting adventures. The next week out of the blue Gary sent Rick a photo of a ship he found and purchased and was currently being refitted in Key West. That was the ship the newly hired captain would run. Rick did have an itching desire to leave that morning and go see it. But they had only been home one day and with the news of Jule's new pregnancy he felt they should chill for a few days before making the trip to Key West. Besides, he was still jetlagged from Africa. He did miss Chief though. Chief, Rick's cute little cockatoo was in Key West with the rest of the crew.

I think I'll call Gary and see how Chief is.

Ring, ring,

"Rick! Did you make it home?"

"Hey Gary, yeah, we're here. Jules is still sleeping. Of crap I'm sorry, I just realized how early it is. I didn't wake you, did I?"

"Wake me? Ha-ha, no, I haven't been to sleep yet. I'm still on Duval Street. I switched from Mojitos to coffee though. I need to drive back to the marina and the last thing I need is a damn DUI. Possum is passed out in my Bronco. He's a lightweight."

"When did y'all begin the Duval Crawl?" asked Rick.

"It actually started on the ship. The new captain, Larry Lane cracked open a bottle of Brugal Rum he had been saving and the next thing you know it was midnight and we were up to our elbows in drinks at Sloppy Joes. Captain Lane took an Uber back around 3:30am and I double dog dared Possum to drink with me until sunrise. You know how he is, well we all are, when it comes to double dog dares. Anyway, he made it and passed out a few minutes after that but I stayed up and met a couple of girls from Tulsa. We went to their resort and had some drinks by the pool. I left and headed back to the Bronco to check on Possum, and he was still snoring away. So, I headed to Banana Café to sober up a little before I drive."

"That sounds like quite a night! How's Chief and everyone else?" asked Rick.

"Everyone is fine. Johnie is supposed be doing a maintenance log on the new ship with Capt. Larry this morning. You know, learning all the systems and most likely trying to get more horsepower out of the diesels. Give him a call. Every time I see him, Chief is on his shoulder lately. They've become quite the pair. I'm beginning to think Chief wants to become a diesel mechanic."

"Ha-ha, okay Gary, drink more coffee and stay safe. We'll probably see y'all in few days."

"You want me to send the jet?"

"Nah, we're probably gonna drive. I ain't hardly put any miles on the new replacement Bronco after I totaled the last one. It probably still has that new car smell."

"Sounds good. Catch y'all later. Bye."

Rick hung up and immediately dialed Johnie.

"Hey Johnie. We're back. How's it going?"

"Hi Rick, were good here,"

Braaaaaaaaawk

Rick heard Chief in the background.

"Johnie, can you switch me to FaceTime?"

"Sure buddy."

"Hi Chief, it's Rick. How you doing buddy?"

Chief leaned towards Johnie's phone as if he was trying to kiss it and his crest rose up and down and he flapped his newly clipped wings.

"You're looking good Chief; your new haircut looks nice. I miss you boy."

Chief bobbed up and down with excitement as the site of Rick's face and his voice.

"Since I got you on Facetime, let me show you around the engine room. This ship was a steal and the engine room is clean as a whistle. The engines have very low hours on them. Gary was smart to buy this. The guy he got it from had no idea what to do with it. The owner was a huge trust fund baby. I don't think he even ever took it out himself. Probably just fancied himself a treasure hunter to impress girls or something."

Johnie flipped the screen around revealing the sparkling white engine room. Johnie walked around with phone and explained that the vessel was equipped with four Cummins KTA 38-M2 engines at 1350 BHP each totaling 5400 BHP. He sat Chief on top of one a handrails and zoomed in on the engines.

"See, no rust or oil anywhere. They look like they were just delivered new in a box," explained Johnie.

"Four engines? Jeez, that's gonna suck some fuel. Are you gonna do any mods?" asked Rick?

"Already have. I installed new chips I created based on my racing days. We will get at least 18% more horsepower and probably a little better fuel economy. The whole damn thing is a write off anyway for Gary. He needs some tax relief. He told me it's incredibly tiring being a millionaire. Ha-ha. I wish I had that problem."

"That Gary is something else. He buys a ship to get a tax break? What a guy."

"Yeah, he's incorporated the ship and is even thinking of taking it public."

"You mean like on the stock market?"

"Yeah, there's another treasure hunting company that went public. It's the ship Odyssey Explorer and they trade on Nasdaq under the name OMEX. They are very volatile and have experienced huge losses historically. That's what Gary wants. He will be the largest shareholder and can write off any losses. Kind crazy but he has an investment guy who's directing him. The same guy who got you to create the Chief-coin crypto. OMEX opened in 2014 at forty dollars a share and have been hovering between three and eight dollars ever since."

"Hmmm, that's over my head but Gary will be Gary," said Rick.

"Wait until you see the sub. It has an ROV and a two-man submarine, plus that crazy dolphin boat. It's called a Sunbreacher and it looks exactly like a bottle nosed dolphin. It does sixty-five miles per hour and can dive and jump out of the water just like a real dolphin. It's insane. We all tried it."

"Yeah, Gary or Possum told me about that. I can't wrap my brain around it. I guess I'll have to see it when I get there. Alright Johnie. Keep up the good work and we'll see y'all in a couple of days, I guess. Ciao for now. Bye Chief!"

"Later Rick," said Johnie as he picked Chief up off of the rail.

Ricks phone vibrated. It was a text from Jules.

> *Hey handsome where'd you sneak off to? Want breakfast?*

> *Morning baby. I'm down in the office. I can come up and make some eggs or we can go out.*

> Let's go to the Pancakery. I'm craving bacon infused pancakes.

> I'm loving your cravings! I'll be right up. I need to put on a decent shirt.

AFTER ASCENDING in the elevator to his condo, Rick freshened himself up, then he and Jules made their way towards the strip mall where the delightful Pancakery awaited them. As usual, there was wait. So Rick put his name on the list, and they walked into Sunsations, a tourist store that sold everything with Destin and the Emerald Coast logos from flip flops to fashion wear. Jules tried to get Rick to try on a few funny hats, but he was having none of it and then surprised her when he put on a pair of dorky sunglasses that looked like two margaritas built into the frame. His buzzer went off and soon they sat at a small table by the window overlooking Harbor Blvd. Jules ordered one Bacon Lover pancake and Rick went for Bananas Foster. They were both stuffed and Rick drank damned near a pot of coffee. As they waddled back to the Bronco feeling overstuffed, they decided to take a walk down Sandprint Drive towards the beach where Rick knew of a public beach entrance. It was about an eight-minute walk and Jules looked stunning in her sundress as her jet-black hair glistened in the morning rays. He was so happy to be with her.

The distance they had traveled together was truly astonishing, from the moment he first encountered her as a dealer in the Virgin Islands to this very moment. It seemed almost surreal to witness their inseparability now, as she gracefully walked hand in hand with him, her womb cradling the precious gift of their child.

Rick had almost forgotten how beautiful the sand was in Destin with its sugar-like appearance that even squeaked when walking on it. The water was spectacular shades of several blues, as little kids used pails to make sandcastles and seagulls glided overhead in search of a dropped chip or other morsal of beach snacks.

They walked to the west almost to Jade East Towers then headed back towards the Pancakery. It was a nice walk and they barely talked as they took in the beauty and serenity that the Destin beach had to offer. It was a glorious start to the day and Rick had plans. He just couldn't tell Jules what they were and needed to sneak away from her at some point. Rick needed to buy a ring. It was time to replace those matching promise rings they bought in Mexico with real diamond engagement rings. His plan was to buy the rings then take the scenic route down to Key West and propose at sunset at Mallory Square with the entire crew in tow. He wanted to make it special for Jules and the rest of his trusted partners and friends. He knew exactly what to say to get away from her. She hated car stuff.

They got back to the condo and Rick decided to start unboxing "Helga One and Two" before he went ring shopping. Once the massage machines were out of the box, he measured them carefully and moved them to the balcony as per Jules wishes. Luckily they had locking wheels and weren't too heavy since the water hadn't been added yet.

"Hey Jules, I need to run to Auto Zone to get some parts for the Bronco. I wanna upgrade the windshield wipers and maybe get some of that new acrylic polish I saw on TV. You wanna come with me?"

"Uhhh no. You go ahead. I'll stay here and do an inventory for food. I'd love to cook tonight. You have a preference?"

"Well, maybe seafood? If you have a dish in mind and know what kind of fish, just text me and I'll stop at Sextons. I noticed when we drove by that they had grouper cheeks on sale."

"Ay Dios mio, yes! I love grouper cheeks. I know exactly

what I'm gonna make. Can you also get some medium shrimp and about a half pound of scallops?"

"Consider it done. I might be a while. I'm picky when it comes to aftermarket auto parts. I may have to go to Fort Walton. They have that four-wheel drive place called Restylers."

Jules rolled her eyes at the thought of Ricks mouthwatering in that 4x4 store.

"Take your time. I feel like being a homebody today."

CHAPTER 2

Rick grabbed his little orange RTIC backpack cooler and threw a couple of ice gel packs in and headed out after giving Jules a kiss on the forehead. He drove straight to McCaskill & Company jewelers and met with the owner. After much deliberation he chose a Kirk Kara "Carmella" 18K White Gold Engraved Halo Diamond Semi-Mount Engagement Ring and matching band for Jules and picked out a "Artin" 18k white gold band for himself. He was happy with his decisions and knew Jules would love hers. He felt bad telling her a little white lie to sneak away, but it was for a little white gold ring after all. Since he made his ring decision so quickly, he decided to go to Restylers like he had mentioned to Jules and get a few goodies for the Bronco for their trip to Key West. He upgraded the head lights and picked up a new set of fog lights and a light-bar. He would install them himself as they couldn't get to him for a few days. It would be a simple task.

After a quick stop at Sextons for the seafood Jules wanted, he returned to the condo and hid the rings in the ceiling of the downstairs office. He was so excited to make Jules his partner for life, he could barely contain himself. Jules was in the kitchen tidying up and doing prep for dinner later. She had already made some nice chicken salad wraps for them to have for lunch. Rick always knew when she made those wraps as he could smell the extra cumin in the air that she always used.

Rick took a huge bite of the wrap as he carried his plate to the dining room table. Jules gave him fake angry eyes then laughed. She dished him out a side of coconut rice and placed a fresh glass of iced tea by him, then sat down with him. Rick devoured his wrap before she was halfway through and with a smile and a head tilt she motioned to him to grab another one sitting in the kitchen. She knew he'd eat two. He always did.

After lunch Jules did the laundry after unpacking their suitcases and disposed of the leftover packaging from the "Helga's" as Rick worked on installing the new fog lights and light-bar on the Bronco.

After finishing the laundry Jules made her way downstairs and saw Rick was polishing his red Bronco in the shade.

"Mine's next!" she said with a laugh.

"Already done bossy! Ha-ha," replied Rick as he pointed at her Bronco glistening in the sun.

"Awe, thank you baby," she said as she kissed him on the cheek.

"What you got going on today except for dinner?" asked Rick.

"I kinda feel like a drive, you wanna join me after you finish waxing?"

"Sure, where to?"

"I don't know. Nowhere special, maybe down 30A. My Bronco has been sitting too long and needs some loving too," she said.

"Sounds good Jules. Maybe we can have a non-alcoholic beer and some fresh oysters at the Hurricane Oyster Bar. It's been a while since we've been there."

"We can play it by ear."

Jules strolled over to her Bronco and cracked the windows as she admired Ricks wonderful wax job. She stopped in the office and curiosity got the best of her. She called a couple of local bail bonds companies to see if there were any bail jumpers that needed to be recovered.

A few months back she had been carjacked while her and Rick were on a case in Mississippi. The trauma from the event affected her greatly and after some therapy she decided that she would never be vulnerable again and took several self-defense courses and got her concealed carry permit. Rick picked her up a nice automatic pistol she kept with her at all times as well as a stun gun and pepper spray for good measure. Her newfound confidence led to a side hustle as a bounty hunter. She found it thrilling and quite lucrative. With her stunning good looks and innocent face, she had the advantage in many cases. No one realized how lethal she could be. Rick never tried to stop, her but as a loving partner, was always concerned and worried.

Most of the jumpers were for failure to appear and didn't really interest her. On her third call to a bond company that tended to take bigger risks and often paid bigger rewards she was told about a guy who was scheduled to be on trial for domestic abuse and attempted murder. He didn't show for his pre-trial hearing and a new arrest warrant was issued for him. The reward for his return was ten thousand dollars. That one interested her. Once she read his case file and found out he had beat his live-in girlfriend so badly that she lost her baby, she knew that was the one she wanted to go after. It made her blood boil.

She downloaded all the photos of the perp, his usual habits and discriminating features. He was two-twenty and had jet black long curly hair with a muscular build. There was a tattoo on his left wrist that caught Jules's eye. She studied it and tried to figure out what it was. The file only said small crown tattoo. She had seen it before and searched her memory, then it came to her. It was a crown for the Latin Kings; a gang from the Chicago area. The only reason she knew about it was because when she was in college, she went to a two-week seminar in Chicago held at the Navy Pier and had met a young Latina girl who was also at the seminar. Being Latina herself, she introduced herself to the young girl and they shared lunch together.

As she got to know her, she told Jules that she had recently left her boyfriend who was an enforcer for the Latin Kings and he made her get the same tattoo on her lower back. She explained how dangerous and jealous he was and was afraid he was going to hurt her. She didn't show up one day for the seminar and then another. Jules found out a few days later that she had been murdered and her boyfriend was wanted for the crime. Her new friend's death shocked and traumatized her, and that crown tattoo was forever embedded into her memory.

Rick stepped in the office and saw the look on her face and knew she wanted to work on a case. He just smiled and washed his hands in the office bathroom and let her do her thing. She zoomed in on the tattoo in the case file and took a screen shot of it with her iPhone. She was gonna get this guy one way or the other. Any member of the Latin Kings in her mind deserved to be in jail. She had lost track of the case in Chicago after she went back to Colombia. That guy was probably dead or in prison by now anyway but the perp she was after now, was still affiliated with the same gang and she felt a drive to get him. It had brought back memories of how she felt when her new friend was found murdered.

"You ready for a joy ride girly?!' asked Rick.

"Let's do it."

She grabbed her keys and purse, and they hopped in her Bronco. She drove and Rick didn't mind at all. As they passed Miramar towards 30-A, he noticed all the new construction and condos going up. The Emerald Coast was growing like a weed. It made him feel a little melancholy. He missed the old little fishing town Destin once was. There was no stopping progress though, and he had to accept it.

Jules drove leisurely down 30-A towards Seaside. They passed the quaint little tourist village of Blue Mountain and Watercolor with its California style villas and condos. Soon they arrived in Seaside and Jules turned into the town circle. The little town of Seaside was used in the film *The Truman Show,* and every time they stopped there it felt as if they were more on a set than in a town. She found place to park, and they strolled in and out of a few shops until they came to The Great Southern Café. It was packed and people were hooting and hollering at the TV which was playing a Florida Gators football game. The excitement in the air was palpable and they decided to join in on the fun. Rick was a Texas Longhorn fan through and through but always enjoyed watching the Gators and their crazy fans who loved to do *"The Chomp."*

Two people were getting up from the small outside bar and Rick quickly took ownership of the coveted spots. The bartender cleaned off the area, as Rick pushed Jules's seat closer to the bar for her, and then sat down.

"What'll ya'll have?" asked the friendly clean-cut bartender.

"You have any non-alcoholic beer? My girl is drinking for two if you catch my drift and I'm supporting her sobriety."

"Good for you man and congrats to you both. Actually, we have a new one that just came out. I tried it and was impressed and I am a beer drinker myself. Do you like IPA's?"

"I do, but Jules would prefer something light."

"Okay for you I suggest the BrewDog Hazy AF. The AF stand for...well, you get it. And for your girl, she would probably enjoy a Suntory All-Free. It's a low-calorie light NA beer. I tell you what if you don't like them, they are on me."

"Sold!" exclaimed Rick.

"Good choice for an afternoon getaway Rick. I love this place. The people are so friendly. I had no idea there were so many non-alcoholic beers."

"Me either. Last time I even heard of one, I think it was O'Douls, which I tried and hated. I'm not even sure they even make that anymore."

Jules took a sip of her beer and nodded a yes and Rick was pleasantly surprised at his with its grapefruit and tropical fruit notes. He loved hazy beers and this one was just as good as any regular IPA he'd ever had. They watched the game and ordered a second round of NA beers and some fried Blue Crab Claws. One guy at the bar was being a bit rowdy and caught Jules attention. He was dark skinned with a bleach blonde buzz cut. He had a mouth like a sailor and was warned a few times by the bartender to keep it down. He was two seats down to Jules's right on the far side of Rick, who was also keeping an eye on him. Rick was a protector. If anyone ever even came close to Jules will ill intent, they would pay a heavy price.

As the man lifted his beer to drink, Jules noticed he was left-handed. He was an angry dude and seemed to be more interested in intimidating the college guys beside him that he was at the game. Jules glanced over at him and noticed he was wearing a red bandana on his left wrist. He could be a Blood although there weren't many gangs in the tourist area. As he took the last sip of his Bud bottle the bandana slid down his arm a little—revealing a tattoo. Her eyes widened and she immediately pulled out her phone and looked at the enlarged tattoo of the perp she was after.

It couldn't be him. What are the odds? she thought.

The guy she was after had long dark black hair, not short blonde. She clicked on his case file and downloaded out the most recent photo of him and scrolled down for any other characteristics.

Jesus Morales
Latino Male
229lbs
35 years old
Latin Kings affiliation
Crown tattoo on left wrist
Small scar above right eye

Last known whereabouts Atlanta area

Jules studied his photos then looked back towards him and gave him a smile. He looked her up and down like a dog staring at a piece of juicy ribeye. As he took her in his gaze, she noticed the little scar above his eye.

Could it be?

She turned away and put her back towards him. Without a word she got up from her seat and unzipped her purse. Rick figured she was going to the ladies room. She slowly walked past and behind the man with the blind buzz cut.

"Jesus?" she yelled in the Spanish way.

He spun around in recognition of his name.

"You are under arrest for failure to appear in Okaloosa County and a bench warrant has been issued for you. I'm taking you in," said Jules sternly.

The look on his face was priceless. He looked down at her and laughed.

"You and what army, pinche puta?"

He leaned back to take a swing at her. She punched him as hard and fast as she could directly in the throat. The force of Jules's strike jolted the perp backward, sending him off balance. Gasping for breath and clutching his throat, he struggled to regain his composure, his eyes filled with a mixture of pain and surprise. Jules seized this opportune moment to take control of the situation, capitalizing on the perp's vulnerability.

With remarkable speed and agility, Jules closed the

distance between them, her muscles coiling like a predator ready to strike. She swiftly planted a firm grip on the perp's wrist, exerting just enough force to subdue him without causing permanent harm. Her keen eyes locked onto his, revealing an unwavering determination.

Using her superior leverage, Jules executed a deft maneuver, defying her opponent's attempts to resist. She spun him around, forcefully pinning his arm behind his back. The Latino man winced in pain as his face contorted, realizing that escape was no longer an option. The once-boisterous bar fell silent, its patrons frozen in anticipation, captivated by the unfolding confrontation. Rick had barely sat his beer down as the incident took place.

Jules maintained a firm grasp, her every movement calculated and controlled. She swiftly reached for a set of handcuffs, expertly securing them around the gang banger's wrists—ensuring he remained restrained. With the battle won, she stood firm, her gaze locked with the defeated bail jumper, leaving no doubt of her triumph. He glanced back at her as she held a stun gun towards his face. He stopped resisting at the sight of it.

Rick jumped up from his seat and helped her drag the guy out of the bar. Only the sound of the game on the TV could be heard as everyone in the bar stood silently and watched the event.

"What the hell Jules? You could've clued me in."

"I wasn't sure and the odds that it was him were bad.

When I called his name, I knew. Then it was too late to say anything. I just reacted."

"Holy shit, don't let me piss you off," said Rick with a chuckle.

He jogged back into the outside bar to pay the tab and let everyone know what had just occurred.

"The tab's on me. That guy has been here twice and he gave me bad vibes. He wasn't good for business and what you and you girlfriend did was amazing."

"It was all her. I just helped her get him to the Bronco. She's one tough chic."

"No shit!" exclaimed the bartender in agreement.

Back at the Bronco, Jules had the man leaned over the hood as a Walton County Sheriff's cruiser pulled up followed by two more. Jules explained who the man was and they agreed to take him in. He gave her the proper paperwork taking over jurisdiction of the man so she could still get paid her reward. As if it was just another day at the beach Jules hopped in the Bronco as Rick approached.

"Hurricanes?"

"Why not."

CHAPTER 3

As Jules drove towards Grayton Beach and Hurricanes Oyster Bar & Grill, the adrenalin began to wear off and she suddenly began to feel tired.

"Would you mind if we skipped Hurricanes and just head home?" asked Jules

"Not at all baby, pull over and I'll drive, okay?"

"Okay."

Rick took the wheel as Jules leaned back in the seat. Maybe it was the NA beer in the sun or the fact that she was pregnant that made her feel so tired. Either way, she could barely keep her eyes open. Rick parked the Bronco and they made their way to their unit.

"Nap?"

"You read my mind Jules."

They snuggled in the bed and although just being that close to Jules made Rick want to fool around, he let her drift off to sleep. He wasn't far behind. They woke up a few hours later as the sun lightly touched the Gulf of Mexico. Jules felt refreshed and after they both brushed their teeth their afternoon nap turned into an afternoon delight.

They both showered and Jules began to prep dinner. She got a text from the bail bonds company that they would make a direct deposit to her account and thanked her for bringing the jumper in. It was a lovely evening and they decided to have dinner on the balcony. The fried grouper cheeks were tender and juicy, and Jules made a special side dish similar to paella but consisted of coconut rice and a special curry.

After dinner they discussed plans to head down to the Keys to check out the new ship and recover the bounty they had tossed from Nine-Tenths before they left for Africa.

Rick relived the story for Jules after she cleaned up the plates.

"After we t-boned that Venezuelan pirate boat, Nine-Tenths was taking on water. We had no choice but to dump the gold after we called for the Coast Guard's help from Key West. We knew there would be an investigation and our share of Mayan Gold we got from the Yucatan would be confiscated."

Rick leaned back in his chair and described the scene to Jules. He described the daunting sight of four men aboard the fast boat, emphasizing the formidable .50 cal mounted turret and the advantage of their Viking's sturdier fiberglass construction compared to the Midnight Express. As the plan unfolded, Rick vividly recalled the crucial moment when he yelled for action. Johnie skillfully maneuvered the Viking, aiming its bow directly toward the port side of the fast boat. With a sudden burst of speed, their boats collided, causing chaos and disarray. The man on the turret was thrown off balance, and before he could regain his footing Rick swiftly ended his threat with a single, fatal shot to the face.

The ensuing exchange of gunfire between Gary, Johnie, and the remaining men on the fast boat intensified. With their boats tightly wedged together, Rick seized the opportunity to retrieve the assault rifles from the fishing net —arming himself and Gary. They unleashed a hail of bullets, tearing through the pirate boat's fiberglass hull causing sparks to fly and further destruction.

As the fast boat continued to spin, Rick had urgently instructed Johnie to reverse their engines. Water gushed into the sinking Midnight Express, and the situation grew increasingly dire. Rick climbed onto the hull, desperately attempting to separate the two boats. Racing against time, he entered the wheelhouse, incapacitated the dead driver, and shut off the boat's engines. The weight of the engines dragged the fast boat down, threatening to pull them under with it.

In a last-ditch effort, Rick had commanded Possum to

release the anchor. As the boat rapidly sank, he struggled to free the anchor from the fiberglass, ultimately succeeding with the force of Johnie's full reverse throttle. With a resounding crack, the bow finally broke free, but Rick's victory came at a price. He stumbled and hit his head on broken fiberglass, blood streaming from his forehead.

Meanwhile, Possum desperately had worked to sever the anchor line before it dragged them down with the sinking boat. In a frantic moment, he resorted to shooting at the line with his .45, finally managing to break it loose, but not without injuring himself in the process. As blood flowed from Possum's face, he anxiously questioned Rick's whereabouts, prompting Johnie to search for their companion, scanning the water and calling out his name with growing concern.

The scene remained filled with debris, the lifeless bodies of the pirates floated face down; fragments of the fast boat surfacing.

"My fate hung in the balance, and left Johnie and Possum desperate for any sign of me amidst the tumultuous aftermath. Luckily, they got me onboard and the rest is history. Then we left for Africa," said Rick nonchalantly.

"You tell that story so well, it almost sounds like a movie scene from a contemporary version of *Pirates of the Caribbean*."

"Sometimes truth is stranger than fiction," replied Rick.

"Do you want head towards Key West tomorrow Jules, or do you need a few more days of rest here?"

"I'll be fine to go as long as we can stop somewhere cool a few times. I don't wanna do the entire fourteen-hour drive in one day."

"Hell no. Me either. How about we stop in Orlando and go to a nice resort with a pool, then we stop again in Miami and check out the newly renovated Ritz-Carlton on South Beach?"

"I like that plan a lot!" exclaimed Jules.

THE AIR WAS crisp and fresh as they turned north on Hwy 330 towards interstate 10 to eventually head south. Destin was on the coast but the drive to Orlando was faster on I-10 than on Hwy 98. They were both excited to get to Orlando. Jules napped part of the way as Rick sipped his coffee from the giant forty-ounce Buc-ee's Mug Jules had picked up for him on a trip to Mississippi a few months back. The drive on I-10 was boring. Just trees, trees and more trees. Once they turned south on I-75 it was only three more hours to Orlando.

They stopped in Lake City at Sonny's BBQ and had lunch. Sonny's wasn't fancy but was a decent chain that was always consistent. Rick always got the *Whole Hog* sandwich; with sliced pork, pulled pork and jalapeño cheddar sausage topped with sweet BBQ sauce on a fresh toasted bun. Jules, as usually, got the brisket sandwich.

They arrived at the Loews Sapphire Falls Resort at Universal Orlando around 2:00pm and checked in.

"Last one in the pool is a rotten egg," exclaimed Jules and she ran into the bathroom to don her black bikini.

She wasn't showing yet and the sight of her in that bikini caught Rick's eye. He threw on his swim trunks and they walked hand in hand towards the pool area. The hotel was exquisite with its s-shaped pool fully equipped with a slide. They picked out two lounge chairs near the slide and kicked off their flip flops to take in the afternoon sun. Jules tried the slide several times as Rick watched her. He was content to sit half submerged at the edge of the pool with his elbows resting on the deck. It was a nice calm relaxing day. They had an early dinner in the hotel and fell asleep before the evening news.

Rick was awakened by a ping on Jules's phone. She picked it up and a huge smile crept across her face.

"Cha-ching!" she chimed.

Rick knew she had just been paid by the bail bonds company.

"Lunch is on you?" asked Rick jokingly.

"Lunch and dinner!" replied Jules.

It was only 9:00am when they hit the road for Miami. Rick called Johnie on the hands free.

"Hey buddy. We're en route, stopping in Miami. We'll be in Key West tomorrow sometime. Anything new to report?"

"All good here Rick. Nine-Tenths is back in the water and has been fully repaired. I did a a few upgrades as we discussed. We took the ship out yesterday on a sea trial and the new engine mods are gonna make you smile. We're all looking forward to y'alls arrival; especially Chief. Possum and Gary are here, you want me to put you on speaker?"

"Sure, go ahead."

"Hey Rick, hey Jules," they all said together.

"Hey y'all. We'll probably arrive tomorrow afternoon. We're stoked to see the new ship."

"Let's do the Duval crawl when you get here," piped up Gary.

"We definitely wanna see Duval but I'm taking a break from drinking. We both are. Let's plan to do sunset at Mallory Square. Sound good?"

"Sure Rick. I'm bet your liver is happy with you even though I'm bummed. Ha-ha," replied Gary.

"Indeed. Alright ya'll. We'll see you soon. Stay out of trouble. Peace!"

"Bye," they all chimed in.

They arrived in South Beach a little after noon. Neither Rick nor Jules had ever been to this Ritz Carlton but had heard how nice they were and since this one was newly renovated; they were stoked to see it.

Rick and Jules arrived at the magnificent Ritz Carlton

Hotel, eagerly anticipating an experience like no other. As they stepped onto the premises, they were greeted by towering palm trees, gently swaying in the invigorating ocean breeze. It was immediately evident that this was no ordinary luxury hotel. They sensed they were about to embark on a journey filled with unparalleled amenities and services, immersing them in a feeling akin to paradise.

After they checked in, they treated themselves to a day at SOAK—state-of-the-art cabanas with rooftop sundecks and exclusive adult-only options. Little did they know that this indulgence would redefine their concept of pampering, transporting them to a state of unparalleled relaxation.

Renowned as one of the finest hotels in South Beach, the Ritz Carlton offered them a plethora of activities and experiences to enjoy—or the option to simply unwind and do nothing at all. They reveled in rejuvenating spa treatment

s at the luxurious Spa. To ensure they didn't miss out on the best attractions in the area, they consulted the Insider's Guide—a comprehensive resource featuring recommendations for unique local experiences within the hotel and throughout Miami Beach. Their stay was exactly what they needed to recharge their batteries.

They decided to head down to art deco district for a Cuban dinner and chose the Cardoza; a place to see and be seen. It was the famous backdrop for a scene in the movie *There's Something About Mary*. The meal was exquisitely South Beach, and they took a stroll down Lincoln Road before catching an Uber back to the resort. They wanted to get an early start for the Keys.

On the early morning drive, Rick decided to take the back way into Key Largo and took Card Sound Road instead of US-1. It was a little slower, scenic route through the mangroves, but Rick liked it better than the bustling highway. They spotted several herons, cranes, and flamingos on the less travelled road into Key Largo. It would take them a little over four hours if they drove straight through.

They made a plan to stop in Marathon and have lunch. Rick wasn't much for tourist traps but he did love lobster, so they pulled into Keys Fisheries to both get one of the famous Lobster Rueben sandwiches. Rick had been there before and knew that instead of giving your name to the window when you ordered you were supposed to use a cartoon characters name, He chose Underdog and Jules went with Polly Purebred.

They were both stuffed as they pulled back on to US-1 for the final leg of the trip to Key West. Ricks sport fisher, Nine-Tenths, was in 3D Boat Yard on Stock Island while the ship was anchored just off of Fort Taylor in Key West. Rick called the gang and asked them all to rendezvous at Nine-Tenths around 1:00pm and take the yacht out to the ship.

When they arrived Rick could see Johnie sitting at the helm on the flybridge with Chief comfortably sitting on his shoulder. He pointed at them both for Jules to see and she grinned from ear to ear. She almost didn't wait for Rick to come to a complete stop before she was opening her door to the Bronco and yelling for Chief. They both jogged up to the stern of the yacht hand in hand. The entire crew was onboard and they were all a sight for sore eyes. Big hugs were shared and Chief was beyond excited as he hopped to Rick's arms, Jules and back. He didn't know where he wanted to be. He was acting more like an excited puppy than a n umbrella cockatoo. He was barking and yipping as usual. Being raised around dogs, he had picked up all their barking and growl sounds.

Possum helped Rick get the luggage onboard Nine-Tenths. Possum had been Rick's best friend since high school and together they had been on many treasure hunting adventures over the years. He had retired early as a professor and now split his time between Rick's new private eye & charter business and his home in Houston. He had a condo. In the same building that both Rick, Gary and Johnie now owned, ever since Gary bought both towers. Gary had come on as a full partner in the P.I. business but Possum was more into the treasure hunting side of things and helping out Johnie on charters. All in all, it was a good team and they all enjoyed each other's company and were close.

Johnie was Rick's first mate. He had hired him right on the spot when he had bumped into him as Johnie was looking at a help wanted bulletin board on Destin's, Harbor-Walk. Johnie an incredible first mate. He was a master diesel mechanic and had run a race team back in Texas before he was banned for developing a new computer engine chip that outclassed the entire field. He now used that same technology on Ricks many boats.

There was a new member of Rick's team; Larry Lane. He was brought on after Gary purchased the massive treasure hunting ship they had yet to christen. Johnie could run the ship but his captains license wasn't yet approved for that tonnage and Larry was already familiar with the ship.

"You ready to hear the MAN's purr?" asked Johnie.

"Fire them up!"

Rick's charter boat Nine-Tenths was a fifty-five Viking with twin MAN diesels engines. Johnie had them finely tuned and upgraded. Since the crash with the Venezuelan pirates and refitting of the yacht, Rick had given Johnie carte blanche to see to the repairs and upgrades as he saw fit. He was excited to get her out on the water. After stowing their bags, he and Jules climbed up to the flybridge with Chief tucked comfortably insides Ricks fishing shirt as usual.

When Johnie fired up the engines, Rick could already tell there was a difference than before the crash.

"I replaced the factory manifolds with stainless ATS Pulseflow manifolds. They are made for racing, but I have a buddy who works at the factory. These are designed for our marine application. They are one-offs. They are using us beta testers before they go to market. They are gonna be called ATS Chiefs. I figured you get a kick out of that."

"Chief is surely impressed!" said Rick with a laugh.

Gary and Possum untied and stowed the lines as Johnie slowly pulled out into the channel. Once he was past the no wake zone, he pushed the throttles forward and the mighty boat dipped down hard, then raised up high and settled on plane faster than ever before. The engines sounded amazing and Johnie pointed at the gauges as he pushed the throttles to the limit. They were going seventeen knots faster than the boat had ever gone before and the RPM's were in the safe zone. Rick couldn't stop smiling as Johnie moved over gave him the helm. Johnie set the course for the anchorage where the ship was and they were there in no time. Johnie took over and slowly pulled alongside the beautiful treasure hunting vessel as he let Rick and Jules take it all in. She was spectacular—complete with a forward landing pad and helicopter.

"Who's gonna fly that?" asked Rick.

"When I first got the idea of buying this, I sent Clay, our jet pilot to chopper school at the Destin Executive Airport. He's almost rated for this one. He's excited to work more closely with us and will be on board soon."

"I hope you gave him a raise," said Rick.

"Duh!" replied Gary.

Gary and Possum set out oversized fenders on the port side of Nine-Tenths as Johnie maneuvered the sport fisher with the twin MANs and bow thrusters to soft landing against the rear starboard side of the ship. The deck was lower about midships, and the freeboard was just low enough to be able to climb off of the sport fisher and onto the ship. That lower deck section is where the ocean toys, ROV and two-man sub were strapped down, along with the crane and rear twin mailbox blowers with fifteen-foot extensions capable of blowing holes in the sand as deep as 45 foot down.

"Welcome aboard!" yelled a gray bearded man.

Rick caught his first glimpse of the new captain, Larry Lane. The captain reached down across the side of the hull and helped Jules on board first. Rick and the rest of the crew followed one by one, right after her.

"It's nice to meet you both, let me give you the grand tour," said Capt. Lane.

"What shall I call you? Captain? Larry? Captain Larry?" asked Rick.

"My friends call me P-Roy. Don't ask me why. They always have. It could be worse. At least my nickname is not Possum," he said with a big belly laugh.

Rick liked Larry right away.

CHAPTER 4

The captain introduced Rick and Jules to the rest of the crew. It took quite a few people to run a ship of this size.

"Rick and Jules, I'd like you to meet the crew. This is Daniel, boatswain, Randy our quarterdeck, Jamie, deckhand and Phillipe our navigator."

"It's nice to meet you all. I'm gonna need to take notes to memorize all your names," said Rick.

"Don't worry, they will all come in time. Don't put too much effort into it. We are signed on with Miami Crewmasters and the crew is changed out every two months. All the crew on our ship are in training. It's a sort of like a paid apprenticeship. It's a win-win for everyone. The crew get experience and we pay less than hiring a full-time crew. It's something I truly believe in. I actually got my start many years ago with a similar program up in Maine. I'll be the only permanent member on the ship. If you decided to keep me." said the new Captain with a wink.

Rick walked behind P-Roy as he pointed out all the finer details on the ship. The way he spoke of the vessel, it was clear he was confident she was uber seaworthy and a strong and mighty ship. His tone had an air of pride. Jules went with Rick on the tour although she was less interested than Rick but did her best to keep up.

"Have you been made aware of what we plan to salvage first?" asked Rick.

"Yes, Gary filled me in and I already signed an N.D.A. I'd like to discuss my contract if that's okay with you?" asked the captain.

"Sure, I have no idea what pay arrangement Gary has discussed with you but if he is in agreement I'm sure it's fine."

"He is, but wanted me to run it by you."

"Okay, let's go sit down in the main salon and talk."

The interior of the ship was more like the inside of a mega-yacht. It was surreal. Being a solid working ship on the outside, you'd never know that by the inside. Soft buffalo leather was throughout and every inch of the interior seemed like they were on the inside of some Italian luxury yacht instead of a real working boat.

Before Capt. P-Roy sat down he poured a Rick and Jules

glasses of cold filtered water from one of the two twin stainless SubZero matching side by side reefers.

"I'd like to forego my salary as a captain for a share of future salvages. I've done well in my years as a captain and when I got here, I had every intention of being just the captain on the generous 175K salary. But after getting to know the crew and really liking everyone, it boils down to one thing. I want to be more than just your captain. I want to be on the team. Possum has one the best minds I've ever had the pleasure of understanding and Johnie is a mechanical genius. I have no skin in the upcoming salvage as that happened before I was involved but I will do that for free in order to show my allegiance and become a full member of your amazing team."

Rick was silent for a minute as he rubbed his chin with his thumb and fingers in thought.

"I tell you what. I will agree to your proposal on one condition."

"Shoot."

"That you become a full team member starting today. Now let me tell you why. Yes, we originally found the Mayan treasure before you were involved but you *are* involved in its recovery. Anything can happen out there and if you wanna be a member then let's start today."

A huge smile crept across Capt. Larry P-Roy Lane's face as he stuck out his hand and shook Ricks with a strong firm grip.

"I understand the sea trial went well. How about another one today?" asked Rick.

"You read my mind boss," said P-Roy.

"Don't call me boss, call me Rick."

"Okay Rick, then call me P-Roy."

P-Roy went up to the helm and summoned Johnie. Gary and Possum secured Nine-Tenths at anchor and reboarded the new ship. The captain gave the sign to raise the anchor as the engines were started and ran at a high idle. Rick joined P-Roy and Johnie on the bridge. Jules went to the bow to enjoy the warm sun and wind as the boat began to make way. Rick kept his eye on a all the digital meters in the wheelhouse. The layout looked more like the cockpit of a modern jetliner than a working ship. Johnie smiled at Rick as he pointed at the speed of the pitometer.

"Twenty-four knots, not bad for a heavy vessel like this. Most cruise ships only average 20 knots. Those four engines you got are really purring!" said Rick.

Johnie started laughing as he pushed two more throttles forward matching the RPMs of the other two.

"That was only two of the engines, look now," said Johnie as he motioned with his head.

"Thirty-six knots! Are you kidding me?" asked Rick.

"She has head room too. I could probably pick up four to five more knots if we needed it. No sense in getting to the redline but it's there," explained Johnie.

"Color me impressed!" explained Rick.

Chief was jumping up and down on Johnie's shoulder —trying to get to Rick—who finally reached over and took him. He was getting overly excited at the drone of the massive diesel engines. Rick rubbed his chest to calm him down. They took her out twenty miles and then deadheaded back towards the anchorage. The engines never even sputtered once and the sea trial went perfectly as planned. It was time to plan the salvage. But first Rick had something he wanted to do at Mallory Square at sunset and kept a close eye on his watch. Once they weighed anchor, Rick asked everyone including P-Roy to join him on Nine-Tenths. The only ones to stay behind were the new crew in training. Someone had to watch the vessel while at anchor. Rick assumed he'd put the quarterdeck in charge once the left the ship.

"Okay, here's the plan. I appreciate the hard work you have all done to get the ship ready for the salvage. I'd like to treat everyone to a nice dinner tonight at my favorite restaurant on the island, Louie's Backyard. I've arranges for a special table to seat us all. But first, I'd like to do the Duval Crawl with y'all. Hey that rhymes. Jules and I won't be drinking as we are doing a sober health kick but I'm buying and by all means indulge all you wish. I'd like us all to go down to Mallory Square at sunset and watch a few of the street performers. Since we have this salvage coming up, I'd like to announce something before we begin the mission and

I think sunset at Mallory Square is the perfect place to do that," exclaimed Rick.

Everyone cheered and went to their cabins to get changed to the upcoming nights festivities. P-Roy even removed his Captains hat and combed his hair. Rick was pretty sure he'd even used Brylcreem in it. He was old school like that. Rick called and arranged for an Uber XL to meet them on Stock Island once Nine-Tenths was side tied to the t-dock. Rick kissed Chief on the beak and put him in his cage up in the flybridge. He thought about bringing him but he was so nervous about asking Jules to marry him, that trying to keep an eye on Chief the entire time would be too distracting. Rick asked the driver if he could stay with them all night. He agreed and they all piled in. A usual, Gary was pregaming with a Busch Light and Possum had obviously had an edible.

They began their journey at Captain Tony's, where they were pleasantly surprised to find an old acquaintance from the past, Micah Garner, performing on stage. They sat back, captivated by his music, and took the opportunity to reconnect. Despite their desire for him to join them, Micah still had three more sets to perform that evening. Rick ensured that Micah included some of the original songs he had composed, such as "Sunshine Billionaire" and "Barstool Sailor," among a few others. After a few rounds each, they walked up the street to Sloppy Joes and the debauchery continued.

Rick continuously looked at his watch and his nervousness caught Jules's eye.

"Are okay Rick? You seem uptight. Maybe you should have a drink. It's okay with me."

"I'm good Jules, I just don't wanna miss sunset at Mallory Square. Keeping these guys on schedule is like herding cats," replied Rick.

"Is it time?" she asked.

"Yeah, we should leave soon."

"Let me handle it."

Jules stuck two fingers in her mouth and whistled louder than the band was playing on stage. Th entire crew and most of the bar for that matter spun around and looked at her.

"Bottoms up boys. Rick's paying the tab. It's time to go. Let's blows this popsicle stand!" she demanded.

They all stood up like little schoolboys and followed her out the door. Rick caught up with her, took her hand and thanked her. She winked at him and smiled.

Once they arrived at Mallory square, the scene was alive with excitement. The usual suspects were there; the juggler, the acrobat and a plethora of other street performers and buskers. Rick was going around tipping them all. Gary and Possum joined in and everyone's tip jar was overflowing. While they all waited for the famous green flash to appear, Rick nervously dug in his pocket several times making sure the rings were still there. Just as the oohs and ahhs ended, he got everyone's attention and got down on one knee. It immediately drew a crowd. The look on Jules' face was priceless as people gather around. Her jaw was hanging open and it was obvious that she was fight back tears. In classic Rick fashion he read a poem he had written.

"JULES, my love, the sea is our guide,
  Together, let's embark on this wondrous ride.
  With you, my heart has found its home,
  Will you be forever by my side, as we roam?"

As WAVES CRASH and embrace the shore,
  Jules you're the one, I can't ask for more.
  If you say "Yes," amidst the ocean's roar,
  Our love, an adventure, forevermore.

So LET our love sail on the tides of devotion,
  Bound forever one with the ocean
  In adventures untold, our spirits take flight,
  If you will just grant me this one small delight.

"JULES, WILL YOU MARRY ME?"
  Tears burst from her eyes, as she yelled, "Yes!" at the top

of her lungs and flung her arms around Rick and kissed him passionately as if no one else was there.

The crowd erupted in applause and even Possum's eyes got watery. The entire crew patted Rick on the back and everyone congratulated them. One of the street performers who Rick had tipped generously showed up out of nowhere with a bouquet of roses and handed them to Jules. Rick had no idea where he got them from so quickly but didn't care. He had his guess that some hotel nearby had an empty vase sitting in their foyer.

They all walked towards Duval together. Several more people hollered out congrats to the couple. There was love in the air and Rick's proposal had created a happy environment for more than just he, Jules and the crew. It was contagious and even complete strangers were smiling. Once back in the Uber, the party and celebration continued. The car arrived a few minutes before Rick's reservation but they were seated immediately. He had arranged for a special meal with all the courses preselected. He pretty much knew everyone's taste in the crew and took the liberty hoping P-Roy wasn't a vegetarian.

The meal started with Bahamian conch chowder with Bird Pepper hot sauce. Followed by seared bacon-wrapped scallops with creamy ravigote & jicama relish. The main entrée's were grilled filet of beef with horseradish crust, red onion confit and twice-baked potatoes. Finally for dessert the waiter brought out chocolate brownie Crème Brulés. It was a feast for a King. After dinner they all returned to Nine-Tenths and had after dinner drinks. Rick and Jules said good-night to everyone. He was not quite done and had one more surprise for her. They climbed in his Bronco and headed back to Key West from Stock Island. He had reserved them an ocean view suite at the newly renovated Casa Marina Resort.

Once in the room, Jules ran to the bed and fell backwards with her arms out to her side.

"Oh Rick, you have made me the happiest woman in the world. Make love to me or lose me forever!" she said.

Rick picked her up in his arms and carried her to the terrace as she kissed her.

"Just look at this view. I feel like an old school romantic."

"You are an old school romantic Rick Waters, you are."

The held each other on the terrace and took in the ocean breeze. The made love to the sounds of the ocean wafting up from below as the palm trees swayed in the breeze. It was a perfect night. The next thing Rick knew, it was morning and they were still as one. He kissed her forehead and made his way to the bathroom to brush his teeth and shower. Before he was finished, he felt her reach in and stroke his back. She joined him under the gentle rainfall shower head and they made love again.

"Feed me!" said Jules with a laugh as they got dressed, then strolled down to the hotel restaurant.

Rick downed two cups of coffee before they even ordered. Jules was eating for two and a got waffles. After breakfast, they took a walk along the shore listening to the gulls laughing and the waves slapping the sand. Jules kept looking at her ring and smiling at Rick. He had never seen her that happy before. He felt the same way. They packed up their overnight bag and drove towards Nine-Tenths. As happy as they were, they both knew it was time to start the salvage.

Rick called Possum who was already on the ship.

"What's the plan hombre?" asked Rick.

"If you two lovebirds are ready, we'll swing by the Marina in the rib and pick y'all up. Gary paid a guy to boat sit Nine-Tenths, so she'll be fine in the marina. This morning Gary put the finishing touches on Chiefs new cage. Hell, it's not a cage, it's a freaking castle. It's built in to the wall. A ten by ten foot complete aviary with a full ocean view. It was that area I showed you that he had taped off and covered with a tarp on the port side of the ship. He called it his pet project. Get it, *pet* project?"

"Ha-ha, very funny. I can't wait to see it. Chief was already squawking when we arrived this morning. He's raring to go," replied Rick.

"Okay, we'll see you in about forty-five minutes."

THE RIDE OUT to the ship was a wet one and they all donned foul weather gear for the ride. The splash of the salt water from the high speed inflatable rib caused by the strong easterly wind kept hitting Rick in the face but he didn't care. It was good to be on the water.

Once onboard the mighty vessel, Rick, Jules and his crew were bustling with excitement as they prepared the new ship for its maiden voyage. The sun's warm rays danced upon the glistening blue waters, setting the perfect stage for this adventure. With their minds set on the tasks ahead, they diligently worked together, ensuring every detail was attended to.

The deck of the ship was a hive of activity, with crew members scurrying about, their hands moving swiftly to secure all the sea toys tightly in their designated spots. The dolphin boat, a symbol of freedom and grace on the water, was carefully fastened to the deck near the stern. Its sleek design and vibrant colors added a touch of whimsy to the ship's exterior. Nearby, the two-man submarine stood tall and sturdy ready to delve into the depths of the unknown. Its gleaming portholes promised breathtaking underwater views to those fortunate enough to board.

As the crew members secured the remotely operated vehicle (ROV), their anticipation grew. This high-tech marvel would enable them to explore the ocean floor with unparalleled precision. Its mechanical arms and high-definition cameras were essential tools for their mission. With the ROV safely in place, they turned their attention to the jet skis. These agile watercrafts were a means of exhilarating transportation, perfect for zipping across the waves or reaching remote locations. Each jet ski was meticulously strapped down, ensuring they would remain steadfast during even the most turbulent conditions.

The helicopter, a magnificent beast of the skies, was a marvel to behold. It sat atop the helipad above the bow, blades poised for flight. Gary had spared no effort in ensuring its secure attachment. They understood the helicopter's value in their exploration, as it provided an unparalleled vantage point and swift transportation to remote locations. Its presence on the ship promised a level of versatility and efficiency that would prove indispensable. They hoped soon Clay would finish his chopper training and join them. The helicopter would be a valuable asset if spare parts were needed or some emergency occurred.

Deckhands scurried across the deck, attending to various tasks. Some were busy checking the ship's navigation systems, ensuring they were calibrated and ready to guide them through uncharted waters. Others double-checked the safety equipment, ensuring that life jackets, flares, and emergency supplies were all in order. A group of crew members prepared the living quarters; ensuring that each cabin was clean, comfortable, and ready to accommodate the weary explorers after a day of adventure.

The ship's chef, aka Possum, armed with an array of culinary delights, busily stocked the galley. The tantalizing aromas wafting through the air were enough to make even the most seasoned sailor's mouth water. Possum wasn't trained as a chef but he knew everyone would be well-nourished during their journey with delicious meals awaiting them after their long days of exploration.

With the sun high in the sky casting a golden hue across the ship, the crew's hard work came to fruition. The ship stood ready, a testament to their dedication and meticulousness. The sea toys were secured tightly, the deckhands had completed their assigned tasks, and every member of the crew had played their part.

Rick and his crew gathered on the deck, their faces beaming with anticipation. The ship, a vessel of dreams and possibilities, was about to embark on its maiden voyage. They knew that this journey would be filled with excitement, challenges, and discoveries yet unknown. With everything secured and safe, they were ready to raise the massive anchor and make way on their first salvage united by a shared passion for exploration and a desire to unlock the secrets of the sea. But there was one problem; they hadn't yet named the ship or christened it. It would be bad luck to head out to sea before doing that. Rick knew he wanted a name that reflected treasure hunting but something but not too on the nose. As if it was magically or spiritually gifted to him, it hit him all at once like a strong beam of light.

"Precious Jules!" he shouted.

"What?' asked Gary looking around not understanding the context of what Rick had said.

"Let's name the ship Precious Jewels but spell Jewels, J.U.L.E.S, he said phonetically.

They all looked at each other and then at Jules as she didn't know what to say and they shook their heads in agreement.

"Yes, *Precious Jules*, it is!" I love it, said Possum.

He ran to the galley and grabbed an extra wide permanent marker and leaned over the side of the bow and wrote it while hanging upside down. He did it to both the port and starboard sides. It looked pretty good considering how fast he did it while inverted. They'd have it painted later. Gary grabbed a bottle of Cristal Champagne from the galley and handed it to Jules.

"Would you do the honors dear?" he asked.

"Me?"

"It is named after you. Who else?"

"That's true," she said as she sheepishly walked towards the bow.

"I christen thee, 'Precious Jules'!"

With a string swing she smashed the bottle against the side of the hull on the bow they all cheered. P-Roy moved the throttles forward and they were underway.

"Let the adventure begin!" exclaimed Rick.

CHAPTER 5

The crash of the sea against the hull sounded like a thunderous symphony of nature's power and fury; its rhythmic assault reverberating through the air. Each wave collided with the ship, unleashing a cacophony of splintering water, spraying droplets that shimmered like diamonds in the sunlight. The mighty vessel quivered under the force; its iron skeleton trembling in response to the relentless onslaught. The crash echoed deep within the souls of those on board, evoking both awe and trepidation, a constant reminder of the boundless might of the ocean. As the sea clashed with the hull; it whispered tales of ancient mariners, of battles fought and conquests won, and the timeless dance between man and the untamed depths.

The captain relinquished the helm to Rick and for the

first time he felt the power of the steel vessel. Chief sat on a rolling wheel-locked perch Possum had built and Jules fed him grapes and watched Rick with tender eyes. The navigator has already set the course Possum had saved in his handheld GPS the day they dumped the Mayan bounty overboard just before the Coast Guard arrived. While their expedition wasn't illegal per say; it was fraught will state, county and federal laws that were tricky at best. It was more of a don't ask don't tell mission. The hired crew, except for the captain had no idea of the true mission and assumed they were on their very first regular treasure hunt expedition. The trip would take a few hours and once they got near the drop, they would anchor nearby but not right on top of it. The depth on the chart in that area was a hundred and forty-five feet. Too deep for scuba so without Nitrox, they'd have to use the ROV to locate the bounty.

As the ship drew closer to the search location, P-Roy took back controls of the ship and gave instructions on how much scope they'd need to anchor at that depth. Once the anchor was secure, Johnie tested all the engines at idle and gave them time to cool down naturally then killed the main engines as the generators took over. The engines had outperformed even Johnie's expectations and he was thrilled. Rick and the gang gathered in the main salon. As much exploration as possible would happen under the veil of darkness. Gary had ordered a portable side sonar for the rib. That way, they could go out after dark and scan the bottom without being detected. They would run without lights and always had scuba gear and spear guns on hand for cover and protection in case they were ever approached by authorities or anyone wishing them harm. It was nearly 10pm when they launched the rib. It wasn't an extremely expensive unit. It was actually mostly used for fishing. But with it's 3D capabilities Gary thought it would be useful. It was a 3D SonarVisualize F3D-S made by Furuno. Gary added two six-volt batteries and a waterproof Windows laptop to the rib to run it. They could get about two and half hours of search time before needing to recharge.

The plan was to start a round square pattern with the rib towing a J.W. Fishers Proton 5 Magnetometer behind them until they got hit on metal then they would switch to the sonar and try to pinpoint the location of the gold. The already knew the general location based on Possum's quick thinking using his portable GPS but with depths near a hundred and fifty feet depending on current they couldn't know for sure where the bounty settled.

They began doing their search pattern around 10:25pm. The moon was nearly full so they could see well. On the rib was Gary, Possum, and Rick. Jules, Johnie and the rest of the crew stayed on board the ship. But Rick kept in constant contact with them via radio and using code words. They had already created a guide for most words. Rick carried a heat-sealed paper with the words:

Fish On = Treasure

Snag = Abort

Shark = Coast Guard

Party = Rendezvous

Oh Shit = *Rescue Us*

POSSUM ADDED the last one to be a smart ass. Rick leaned against the console of the inflatable rib, squinting at the magnetometer's display. The moon's bright rays shined down on him, intensifying the excitement that coursed through his veins. The crew had spent months researching and planning this expedition, and now he was finally out on the water, ready to unearth the lost treasure.

The magnetometer, a device capable of detecting anomalies in the Earth's magnetic field, was the key to their mission. Rick had spent countless hours studying its readings and knew that if they followed the signals it emitted, they would eventually stumble upon the gold. Beside Rick, his partner and best friend, Possum, manned the twin outboard engine, skillfully maneuvering the rib through the deep dark waters. Both men were dressed in skins, ready to climb in the water of need be.

As the minutes turned into hours, Rick's anticipation grew. The magnetometer's rhythmic beeping guided their course, urging them onward. They had been scouring the area for nearly two hours, and Rick couldn't help but wonder if all their efforts would be in vain. But he couldn't give up;

he had invested too much time and energy into this adventure.

Just as Rick was about to suggest a change in direction, the magnetometer's pitch shifted, indicating a stronger magnetic anomaly. A surge of adrenaline shot through him as he relayed the news to Johnie on the ship. Johnie returned a big Texas 10-4, their determination renewed.

With renewed vigor, they followed the magnetometer's signal, inching closer and closer to the epicenter of the anomaly. The water around them grew rougher, swirling around them by their passage. Rick's heart raced with anticipation, his eyes darting around, searching for any sign of their elusive treasure on the screen on the 3D sonar.

Then, out of the murky depths, a glowing red silhouette began to materialize on the screen. It was an unmistakable shape, slowly revealing itself to be the tail section of an aircraft. Rick's mind raced as he tried to make sense of what he was seeing. A plane wreck was not what they were expecting, but it held its own allure. The wreckage was undoubtedly that of a DC-3 airplane. The massive tail section sat on the ocean floor like a monument to the past.

"A freaking plane?!" asked Rick.

"Yeah, I wasn't expecting that," added Possum as Gary nodded in agreement.

The rib circled the wreckage, their minds imagining how it arrived at its final resting place, trying to piece together the plane's history. Rick couldn't help but wonder what had brought the aircraft to such a watery grave. Had it crashed during a storm? Or was it the result of a deliberate evasive maneuver done by drug dealers?

Time seemed to stand still as they explored the wreckage on the screen, their minds filled with questions. Rick's fascination with treasure momentarily shifted to a deeper appreciation for the mysteries that lay beneath the surface. After what felt like an eternity, they marked its location, but couldn't help but feel a tinge of disappointment. The treasure they sought had eluded them, yet they had stumbled upon a different kind of treasure—one steeped in history and intrigue.

Rick looked back at the wreckage on the screen one last time, silently promising himself that he would return to uncover its secrets. As they steered the rib back towards the ship, he couldn't help but feel a renewed sense of purpose. The journey was far from over, and he knew that the next chapter of their adventure would be even more exhilarating.

Little did Rick know that this unexpected discovery was only the beginning of a series of revelations that would change the course of their treasure hunt. The tail section of the DC-3 airplane was just a stepping stone, a clue that would lead them deeper into the realm of mystery and adventure.

With the taste of the unknown lingering in their minds, Rick and the guys headed back to the ship to recharge the system, ready to chase the secrets that lay hidden beneath the waves. The ocean beckoned, promising both treasure and a thrill that could only be found in the uncharted territories of their imaginations.

Rick put his finger across his lips signifying to Gary and Possum to stay quiet about the find. There were crew on board that didn't need to know every single detail of the hunt. He would let, Johnie, Jules and the captain in on it but for now, the rest had to think the first run was a bust.

"Here, take this," said Gary as he handed Rick the laptop.

"Let's meet on the bridge and go over the scan together," said Rick.

Possum and Gary hooked up the batteries on the rib to a fast charger and caught up with Rick and the in-the-know crew in the bridge.

"It's definitely a DC-3 tail. No doubt about it. There's no telling how long it's been down there," said P-Roy.

"What's that squiggly line where the tail is broken off that goes all the way across the screen?" asked Rick.

"That's a shelf. The damn shelf. Where the Florida Straits end, and the Continental Shelf begins. You see this side of the line is between one-forty-five and one fifty?" asked Gary.

"Yeah, and?" asked Rick.

"Look closely at the other side of the line."

Rick leaned closed and squinted.

"It says 1000F. A thousand feet?" asked Rick.

"No, it's a thousand fathoms, or approximately six thousand feet. We dropped the gold on the edge of a deep ledge. Let's pray it's on the shallow side!"

"So, that old tail dragger plane is sitting on the edge of the outer continental shelf? And the rest of it?" asked Rick but he already knew the answer.

"Deep my friend, very deep."

"How deep can our sub go safely?" asked Rick.

"The Ocean Pearl is rated to 380 meters or about 1250ft. so it's safe to go to the edge of the shelf but there's no way we can get to the sea bed after the drop. The ROV can do it. That may be our only choice if the gold did fall off the edge," said Gary.

They all synchronized their watches and waited for the batteries on the inflatable to recharge. Possum was already drawing sketches and trying to find a way to get more work time from the battery powered sonar and magnetometer.

"I got it!" he hollered, catching everyone off guard.

"What? Herpes?" asked Gary sarcastically.

"Maybe, that shit is everywhere, ha-ha. But seriously. If we can add two more six-volt batteries in series and add a regulator rectifier to the outboards and wire them together, we can use the engines to charge the external batteries. Theoretically, you should be able to work non-stop."

"Where can we get one of those? Key West?" asked Rick.

"Damn, I wish Clay was finished with his damn helicopter training. He's got to be getting close. We have it just sitting there and no way to fly it." said Gary.

"I have an idea. Do you trust me, Rick?" asked Johnie.

"Goes without saying."

"Remember that kid I told you about when you were in Africa that helped me bring Nine-Tenths to Destin? Well, he also mated back with me to Key West when we decided to bring her there. I really wanted him to be on the team for the ship but he was working another job and couldn't commit. I spoke with him yesterday and he left his position on the mega-yacht because they were going to the Med and he was raised there and wasn't interested in returning to Greece. His name is Sebastian, Sebastian Pappas, like the restaurants in Houston but no relation. Anyway, to make a long story short. He asked me if there was any work for him here and it just dawned on me. He is one of the most talented runners I have ever known. If you need something like a part or something odd, if it's on the island, he will find it. Plus, he knows how to run Nine-Tenths single handed. I could call him and ask him to bring two new six volts and that regulator rectifier thingamabob and he could run them out to us on Nine-Tenths. He could be our Greek Gopher for now until Clay can join us and we use the chopper. He was in the Greek military, the Hellenic Air Force. I'm not sure what he did for them but he has sort of a Possum mind. He'd be a great asset for us. He can figure out anything. He also knows where I hide the spare keys for Nine-Tenths," said Johnie.

"Okay call him."

Johnie ran down to his cabin and returned a few minutes later.

"He's on the hunt for the parts. And he said he'll text me when he's en route."

"It's almost midnight. There are no stores open," said Rick.

"I didn't say they would be new parts."

Rick stuck his fingers in his ears made the la-la-la humming sound as if he didn't wanna hear.

"He's on his way. Just so you don't worry, he didn't steal them. He called a friend who owns a repair shop in Stock Island and they borrowed the stuff from one of his refits. They were gonna toss the stuff anyway and it's in perfect working order he said. They tested the batteries and they took a full charge," said Johnie.

"This should work perfectly. The other batteries should be fully charged when he arrives and we can at least get a nice long scan done before sunrise. If this keeps up, we may have to split up into shifts. We have to sleep sometime," added Rick.

The unmistakable sound of the MAN engines caught Rick's attention, so he went up to the bow to see his beautiful sport fisher gliding across the deep blue. He had never seen it from that angle as he was usually on the dock in

Destin as it approached. It looked spectacular. The rest of the crew headed up and Sebastian slowly pulled Nine-Tenths alongside. Rick reached down and helped him up with the parts.

"Nice to meet you Sebastian, I am Rick Waters. Thanks for doing this. We'll take care of you."

"The pleasure is mine Kýrios Waters. I mean Mr. Waters. You have to excuse me, I slip in and out of Greek far too much. I've only been in states for two years after leaving my military post."

Sebastian hugged Johnie like an old friend and Johnie introduced him to everyone. He was in his early thirties with curly black hair and a slender muscular build. He looked younger though and could easily pass for his mid-twenties. Possum explained to him what he wanted to do and instead handing the parts over to him, he climbed on the rib with a small rolled up tool bag he also had under his arm. Since he removed it from one boat, he knew exactly what tools he'd need to put it on another. After Johnie passed down the new, used six-volts he got to work and knocked it out in under ten minutes. With his tester he stood up a with huge smile and gave the thumbs up.

"Ekató tois ekató, a hundred percent!" he yelled.

Johnie helped him back on the ship and asked him if he minded staying on board until morning. He agreed without further discussion. Some of the hired crew attached a towing hawser to the stern of the ship and the bow on Nine- Tenths and left if drift about sixty feet behind the ship, out of harm's way in case heavy seas developed. Once Nine-Tenths was secure, Rick, Gary and Possum again began a sea scan.

After several hours of scanning there were no new findings. They were all beginning to realize that it was a distinct possibility that the gold had fallen off of the edge was sitting somewhere around six thousand feet. It would make the salvage incredible more difficult. The sun had not quite peaked above the dark blue horizon when they called it off for the day.

Jules had prepared a carb loaded breakfast, she never slept a wink as her man and the guys were out on the inflatable. She was far too worried. Now that everyone was back safe on the boat she relaxed and had herself a cup of coffee. She felt a pain in her stomach. At first it was like light stabbing sensation. She ran to the closest head and felt light headed as she closed the. door behind her. Rick noticed her distress and followed behind her, but gave her some privacy.

"You okay Jules?"

She didn't answer. He knocked and called her again.

"Jules, Jules, are you okay?"

Still no answer.

He reached for the handle of the door and turned it. She hadn't locked it. When the door opened, he saw her laying on the cold floor. There was a little spot of blood on the toilet seat and her leg. He knelt beside her and took her head in his hands. She was out cold. He softly patted her cheek.

"Jules, wake up, wake up."

He felt for a pulse and she was breathing but it was shallow.

"Help me! There's something wrong with Jules." yelled Rick.

Several of the crew helped Rick get her to the couch. She had a small bump on her head and she was still unconscious.

"She needs a doctor now. Dammit! I wish Clay was here to fly that damn chopper. It's gonna take over two hours to get her to Key West on Nine-Tenths," exclaimed Rick.

"I can fly her," injected Sebastian.

"What? Fly her?"

"Yeah, I flew H215 Airbus choppers in Greece. I'm sure I can fly that tiny whirlybird you have on the deck. Meet me there in five minutes."

Rick and the rest of the crew had stunned looks on their faces as they helped Jules to the deck. She had come to a little but was extremely dizzy and disoriented. Sebastian was sitting in the pilot seat with the manual open and looking over the dials, knobs and buttons of the helicopter.

"Good news. It's made by Airbus and it's not that much different than my military chopper, just smaller and fancier. Same concept. No problem."

Rick motioned to Possum to come with him. He might need his help at the hospital. The sun was just about to peak as the chopper blades began to slowly spin. Sebastian appeared confident to Rick as Possum climbed up in the seat next to him with Rick in the back cradling Jules. The chopper rocked a little then lifted off. Out of the port side windows Rick could see Cuba as they gained altitude and soon enough the shape pf Key West came into view.

"Key West approach 96 Whisky Charley. We have bravo Key West. We have a medical emergency and need clearance for Lower Keys Medical Center"

"Turn 96 Whisky Charley, Key West approach, there is no tower, you are on your own ATC, copy? Helipad occupied."

"10-4 Key West Tower, we will take the parking lot. Out!"

Rick over head the conversation between Sebastian and the tower and when he saw him turn down the radio he knew he was a guy they could use in the future. He was fearless. The lot was mostly vacant as Sebastian approached. He softly sat down and Possum and Rick carried Jules into the emergency room. The staff put her in a gurney and rolled her into the back. She was barely conscious. Rick paced the floor wringing his hands constantly waiting for the doctor to come out. Outside Sebastian was doing his best to explain to the Monroe County Sheriff's deputies why he landed in a parking lot. He was using more Greek than English trying to frustrate them enough not to arrest him. He didn't have his ID with him and gave them a fake name which would give him time. Finally, after an hour the doctor came out.

"Are you Rick Waters?"

"Yes, how is she."

He motioned for Rick to come over.

"Hi Rick, I'm Doctor Neil Cummings. Your fiancée Jules will be fine. She couldn't stop talking about your recent engagement. Congratulations. She has a small concussion where she banged her head on the tile floor. She's more embarrassed than anything. That's why I called you over to talk privately. She told me she hadn't eaten for a while and when she got a pain in her abdomen she went to the bathroom. That is when she realized she had gotten her period. She said when she stood up too fast from the toilet she got dizzy and fell, hitting her head on the tile. But other than the concussion she will be fine. We'd like to keep her for a night to make sure there is no brain swelling. Concussions are usually fine but it's better to be safe than sorry. She's conscious now if want to see her. She was asking for you."

"Thank you doctor,' said Rick as he shook his hand with a firm grip.

Rick walked over to Possum and told her she just had a small concussion.

"They are keeping her overnight. I'm gonna go see her now. Why don't you see if you can help Sebastian and get that chopper out of here before he loses his license or something. Just take it back to the ship and I'll stay with Jules. If they release her tomorrow, we can decide then how to get back to the ship. We should probably use Nine-Tenths and lay low with the helicopter for a while. Good luck buddy."

Rick made his way to Jules' room. She smiled then covered her face as if she was embarrassed when he came in.

71

"There's nothing to be embarrassed about Jules. I'll keep it between us."

"I'm not pregnant after all. I *was* late, and the doctor said sometimes those pregnancy tests give false positives. They tested me here and confirmed I am definitely not pregnant. Do you still wanna marry me?" she asked with pouty puppy dog eyes.

"Of course, I do baby. More than ever. As a matter of fast I spoke with the captain on Precious Jules and he said he can marry us. How about we go to the county courthouse after they release you and get the paperwork."

"Get married at sea? I'd love that. And all your friends will be there. I sure wish my mom and dad could be here. They'd be so proud."

"Maybe we can do a second ceremony in Colombia?" asked Rick.

"That's sounds great. I'm so happy you are here. I'm so embarrassed."

"Now you just stop that! Put it out of your mind. We'll never speak of it again. You stood up too fast and got dizzy and fainted. It's called orthostatic hypotension aka low blood pressure and extremely common."

She smiled and squeezed his hand.

"I guess we can try again if you want?"

"I'd sure love to practice a lot," said Rick with a wink.

CHAPTER 6

Possum munched on a bagel on Precious Jules in the galley and wove the tale of how he and Sebastian had outwitted Key West's finest. He was laying it on thick as only Possum could do, and had the entire crew hanging on every word. Even Sebastian was wide eyed as he listened even though he was right there when it happened.

"Alright, gather 'round, mates! I've got a tale to tell ya, a true adventure that unfolded not right over yonder in Key West. It was just me, ol' Possum, and my new trusty sidekick, Sebastian, ready to outsmart the Key West Sheriff's Department.

Once I knew Jules was okay, I left Rick and joined Sebastian who was already speaking in both Greek and English to the deputies. They looked extremely frustrated and confused. I knew I had to be cunning, so I put my resourceful mind to work and hatched a plan.

Sebastian, I whispered, we're gonna need a bit more of that Greek flair and some quick thinking to pull this off. With a sly grin, he started rattling off words in Greek and pointing at the sky.

I explained that the hospital parking lot wasn't busy, and was the only reasonable safe spot for us to land, since the helipad was already occupied. With precision and nerves of steel, Sebastian had guided the chopper toward the destination, and made a perfect landing. The cops were still upset though.

Now, here's where our plan truly took flight, excuse the pun. I motioned for one of them to follow me over to the flight deck and grabbed the radio, my voice steady and authoritative. Channeling the air traffic control tower, I transmitted coded messages, making it sound as professional and serious as possible, but got no response. And Sebastian, well, he truly embraced his Greek side acting in a manner that would make Zeus himself proud.

I showed the deputies that we had unexpected radio failure and weren't transmitting or receiving, a problem that could befall even the most experienced pilots. The truth was Sebastian had turned down the volume. I explained how we had no choice but to make an emergency landing at the hospital parking lot for safety reasons, and to get Jules help. I spun the story with such conviction, such believability, that it left no room for doubt. The authorities couldn't help but buy into our tale, as it seemed like a plausible turn of events.

They honestly didn't know what to do. They all kind of gathered around one of the cruisers and talking amongst themselves, and then the tall one just waived us off with gesture and the back of his hand in frustration.

The chopper roared to life, and with a final glance at our surroundings, we soared back into the skies and back here, leaving behind a story that would be whispered among the Key West Sheriff's Department for years to come. That, my mates, is how we outsmarted the authorities, dodged any pesky tickets, and managed to take off once more without involving the FAA. It was a daring adventure. The End. Ha-ha!"

"Bravo! Bravo!" voiced the crew.

With Rick still at the hospital and under full sunlight, Possum asked Gary if he'd accompany him to get acquainted with the submarine. The Ocean Pearl 1250 was a private two-man submarine built for adventure. They both climbed inside and Possum read aloud from the owner's manual.

The Ocean Pearl is an exceptional manned submersible for two souls, designed for quick deployment, whether from the shore or offshore. Unlike traditional submarines, this model boasts an incredibly shallow draft, allowing it to navigate on the water's surface even in very shallow areas. It can be easily transported on land using a trailer and can even be launched from shore using a regular boat ramp. One remarkable feature of the Ocean Pearl is its clamshell-like cabin, which opens fully in half, providing a spacious entry and exit hatch for easy access.

Versatility is a key characteristic of the Ocean Pearl, as it is highly modular and can be outfitted with a diverse range of subsea tools to tackle various underwater tasks. Equipped with robotic manipulator arms, camera systems, sonars, and acoustic imaging equipment; this submersible possesses both power and agility. It also boasts a comprehensive underwater navigation system comprising DVL, USBL, INS, GPS, and surface tracking equipment; ensuring precise underwater positioning and facilitating precise survey grids.

Despite its compact size, this small submarine possesses significant spare buoyancy ballast, enabling efficient payload recovery. Furthermore, it excels at maintaining a fixed position, making it ideal for underwater intervention work. The Ocean Pearl is a highly effective submersible that requires only basic maintenance. Its core systems are engineered to be kept in their simplest form, ensuring that the vessel can be easily maintained by the operating crew.

"Let's take it for a spin," said Possum.

"Are you nuts? Rick's not even here."

"It's a two-man sub, three's a crowd. I'll text Rick and see what he says."

Rick, how is Jules?

She's good, Stable and will probably be released tomorrow.

Good to hear. Do you mind if Gary and I test out the

submersible? I checked the radar and there are no vessels within twenty miles of us.

Okay, sounds good. Be safe and if anyone approaches, just stay submerged.

Got it. I'll keep you posted.

They both climbed out of the sub, and Possum got his Canon camera and several lenses. Gary put together a small cooler with bottled water and two Busch Lights. There was no way he was going to do his first submarine ride without a beer.

Once the crew got them into the water with the crane, they motored around on the surface a while and made sure they had radio contact with the helm. It was a simple machine to operate. With Possum at the controls, they slowly submerged just a few feet below the surface as he got used to steering it. It glided nicely under the surface. Using the GPS coordinates he had saved for the crashed DC-3 plane, he slowly guided them towards it. Several schools of yellow-tail snapper and other fish came along for the ride. Gary snapped photos with Possum's Canon after a quick on the spot lesson. It was just set to AUTO. As they got deeper and deeper it got darker and he turned on the powerful lights. The ocean came alive in the lights beams. At about a hundred and ten feet down, the plane's tail began to take shape as they approached.

Possum slowly guided it towards the wreck and circled it several times. Gary snapped photos as fast as he could. With grace and agility Possum steered the sub towards the massive gap where the tail had separated from the main fuselage. They were hovering at a hundred and fifty feet with six thousand feet below them to the ocean floor. Gary began to sweat with nervousness.

Possum got as close to the opening as he could and aimed the lights inside as Gary took photos. Inside the cone of the tail were piles of canisters covered in cargo mesh. From the looks of the growth on the tail, it hadn't been down there very long. The numbers on the tail were HK-1966. Possum knew immediately that those numbers signified a plane from Colombia. He also knew that the cargo on board could very well be drugs. With careful precision he backed away from the gaping hole of the plane and over the dark abyss.

"Wanna go deeper?"

"Uh, no. I'm good. We are only rated to 1250ft and even if we took her to the limit we would be anywhere close to the bottom of the shelf. I say we head up and call it a success."

"Chicken, bock-bock."

"Call me whatever you want, I'm ready to ascend," implored Gary as he cracked open a Busch Light.

Possum just shook his head.

"Alright, alright, alright," said Possum imitating Mathew McConaughey as he started to ascend.

Soon they surfaced and were lifted onto the ship by the hydraulic crane. They climbed out and made their way to the main salon to look at the photos and video. Gary wasn't aware that Possum had inserted a flash drive into the onboard video camera system of the sub and was pleasantly delighted. It even had audio. Possum joked that he could even hear Gary sweating. The lights really brought out the colors of the fish as the descended on the video. Possum did a Google search for the plane's tail numbers and it was indeed a Colombian plane. The last known flight path had it landing in the Bahamas on a private island. It was eventually reported missing and a flight plan leaving the Bahamas was never filed. Whoever was flying it was most likely heading back to Colombia and didn't want anyone to know. That made him doubt that the cargo was drugs. It would be going the wrong way.

"We need to use the ROV. It's too deep for scuba and we need to try and raise one of those canisters. It will be tricky because the tail is teetering on the edge of the shelf and any sudden movement could send it over the side. We need to be able to cut the cargo netting and pull out at least one of the canisters and somehow get a float on it. Who is the best at video games here?"

Sebastian raised his hand.

"I have high score on Galaga at The Retro Room in Key West. I also know my way around most aircraft and chopper cockpits. I can do damn near anything with a joystick."

"We will need to use the arms of the ROV to cut the cargo netting and secure an inflatable lift bag on one of the canisters, then pull it out and raise it. It will also need to be done at night. It won't make a difference under the surface but we don't wanna retrieve a giant canister of coke and get nabbed by the Coast Guard. We have no idea what's in those cases and we need to keep it on the down low until we do. Agreed?"

"Agreed they all said."

Only the team was allowed in the salon if they were having a meeting. The hired crew knew when to stay away and not eavesdrop. Johnie always made sure the area was secure when discussing any missions. He took it upon himself to sort of be the security detail for the team. It was easier for him since he relayed most of the orders to the hired hands from the captain. Sebastian was the odd man out that was allowed and although he didn't know it yet he was about to become a full team member. Rick made that clear after how well he handled himself taking Jules to the hospital. He was a valuable asset.

"I know we are all exhausted not having slept. Let's all get a few hours shuteye and meet back here at 19:00 hours. We can have dinner and go over the next dive," said Possum.

They all retired to their quarters except for Sebastian. He didn't have a room yet and wanted to familiarize himself with the ROV controls. He read the manual twice and activated it to test the mechanical arms and other onboard tools. It was technical and didn't function well out of water but he at least knew what all the controls did. It had a hydraulic cutting arm with something akin to metal shears. He tried it on an old piece of towing line and it cut through it like butter. He was certain it would work well to cut the cargo mesh. He tried to rest on the large leather couch in the main salon but never fell back to sleep. He made a peanut butter and jelly sandwich and rested his eyes afterwards. His mind was racing and all he could think of was running the ROV and every possible hitch he might run into. There could be current, equipment failure, predator engagement. The possibilities were endless. He tried over and over to visualize a successful salvage but the snags kept popping up in his head.

Eventually he drifted off for about an hour, but he was awakened by someone dropping a pot or pan in the galley. He glanced down at his watch and saw it was already 6:00pm. He decided to get up and wash his face for dinner. The way Rick had set up the ship meals was smart. Breakfast, lunch and dinner were all served at specific times. If you wanted to attend and get fed, there was a board with your name on it and the corresponding dates, all you had to do was check mark your name if you were eating. That way food wasn't wasted and provisioning could stay accurate. Everyone on board had a plastic cup and a separate coffee cup with their names on it. You were responsible to getting your own beverages. If you chose to miss a meal, or attendance wasn't possible, peanut butter and jelly sandwiches as well as deli meat and cheese sandwiches were available twenty-four hours, self-serve. It made for smooth operation and meals were often shared together, making it more enjoyable and a way to stay close during salvages.

At 7:00pm on the dot, the meal bell sounded off. Today's main protein was sea bass and Possum had prepared it perfectly with a chargrill flavor and mango salsa. It was served with a garden salad and spicy Texas style rice pilaf. Everyone gathered around the main dining room table which was oval and seated fifteen. All were there at the with the exception of Rick and Jules who were still in Key West at the hospital.

"How's the fish?" asked Possum.

Some answered with positive remarks while others only nodded as their mouths were full.

"You missed your calling Possum. You could've been a master chef in a five-star Michelin restaurant," said Gary.

"I love to cook but I'm not sure I'd enjoy the pressure of running a kitchen in a restaurant. Besides I have to do all the critical thinking for you numbskulls on board," he laughed with a half a mouthful of salad.

The talk soon turned to Rick and Jules.

"When are they returning?" asked Sebastian.

"I'm picking them up after dinner. Jules didn't have any brain swelling, just a bad headache and she will need to take it easy for a while. All in all, it's good news. We'll probably be heading back here as y'all are getting the ROV in the water. I know for a fact he's keen to see how it works," replied Johnie.

"What's the max depth of the ROV?" asked Gary.

"According to the owner's manual and everything I could find online, the Perry XLX can go down to four thousand meters or about thirteen thousand feet which is more than double the operating depth we will be at. I messed around with the grabber and cutter arms and I think we will be just fine," replied Sebastian.

"Are you ready to explore the deep waters, Sebastian?" asked Possum.

"I'm stoked. I'm a little nervous because I can't even imagine how much that thing cost."

"I can tell you that it came with the ship. But the replacement cost of it is ten times your annual salary. Don't worry, if you crash it, you can just make payments on the new one. Ha-ha," said Gary.

"Great!"

Once the plates and dishes were cleared from the table, Sebastian and the others went to the deck where the ROV was secured to the crane, and they began to lift it over the starboard rail into the deep waters. Johnie had already untied from the ship and was en route to Key West. He planned to pick up Rick and Jules near Mallory Square.

Once the ROV was in the water, Sebastian ran it just below the surface, to get used to the controls. It had its own GPS and he set it to dive a few yards in front of the sunken DC-3 tail and hover. It took nearly an hour and a half for it to safely descend, then a beep sounded acknowledging its location. They all gathered round as Sebastian steered it manually closer to the plane section. Once he got close to the opening of the tail, he turned on the powerful LED lights and it lit up like the fourth of July. Carefully he steered the ROV inside of the plane. On the screen there were lots of small fish darting back and forth across the beams of light. He tried to use the thrusters with small quick bursts so as not to kick up sediment.

Soon he was within a foot of the cargo net. He used the left grabber arm and slowly clamped onto the net. He was secured and stable, then he used the right cutting arm to cut through the cargo net. It was tedious work and sweat was dripping down his face. Once ten cuts were made there was enough room to reach inside the netting and try and secure one of the cases. As he gripped it and used his reverse thrusters the entire load lunged forward and fell kicking up a huge cloud of sediment. The screen went dark and he lost his visual feed for a minute. One of the cases had fallen out of the cargo net and knocked the port side light out. Once the sediment settled a little, he adjusted the starboard light and was able to clearly see the pile of cases.

He slowly reversed and the entire tail shifted. It was preciously sitting on the edge of a huge drop. It appeared that maybe about fifteen cases were inside of the tail section. He slowly reversed back and gently hovered about two inches off of the tails bottom. The thrusters were kicking up sediment but most of it flowed out of the tail into open water which made the visual slowly get clearer. With the precision of a brain surgeon, he clamped onto the handle of the flight case. He slowly dragged it towards the edge of the tail. Once he was about a foot from the edge he carefully pushed the D-ring forward until it clipped into the handle.

"Phew!" he sighed.

All he had to do now was to execute perfect timing. He had to pulled the case out of the tail and simultaneously click a button that would release the co2 cartridge and fill the lift bag attached to the case. If his timing was too slow, the case could fall and pull the ROV down to the ocean floor. But if he was too fast, the lift bag could fill up inside of the tail and possibly cause it to rock and fall over the shelf.

"Here goes nothing," he said under his breath.

He pulled the case right to the edge and it teetered for a second and then began to fall, that instant he pushed engage on for the co2 cartridge. The lift bag quickly began to fill and rise but he was still caught on the gripping arm and the lift bag pulled the ROV to the ceiling of the tail causing it to slam hard. He quickly hit full reverse and opened and closed the claws trying to disengage from the lift bag's tether. With one more hard reverse thrust, the line finally slid off and the case flew past the screen and quickly ascended past the ROV. Gary and Possum stood by waiting for the signal in the inflatable with search lights. Johnie used his arm to direct them to the general direction the lift bag should surface, and they motored slowly that way scanning the water's surface.

Everyone on deck cheered at the sight they had

witnessed on the screen Sebastian was operating. Gary yelled as he spotted the yellow float on the surface and without ever using their flood lights, and guided by the strong moonlight, they pulled the black aluminum flight case on board and with Possums help deflated and rolled up the lift bag. Gary spun the inflatable around and climbed onboard Precious Jules as Possum handed him the case. The crew secured the inflatable to the crane and sat it on the deck. Sebastian used the return home function and the ROV began to ascend to the area they had started. The ship had barely moved in the current from where it was anchored and the ROV popped up a few yards off the stern. He slowly motored it close and soon it was secure to the crane lifted on board safely as well. The mission was a complete success.

"What is it?" yelled Sebastian.

"We're about to find out," replied Gary.

He sat it on a heavy aluminum work bench secured to the starboard rail and hosed it off with fresh water. Possum used some large towels to dry it off. Captain P-Roy gave the all clear that no vessels were within ten miles of the ship and then turned on the powerful deck lights, so they could see better. Gary took a deep breath as they all gathered around and slowly turned the semi-crusted latches of the case. The aluminum had a small amount of pitting, but not a lot indicating that the cases hadn't been down there too long. Once he unsnapped the last latch, he slowly opened it. As everyone stood there holding their breath, he revealed the bounty. Inside sat a large heavy black plastic bag. He pulled out a pocketknife and carefully cut into it.

With both hands, he pulled apart the bag exposing its contents. It was silver and shiny and immediately identified as a commercial scale. He pushed it aside and grabbed a heavy black object and pulled it out. It had a small keyboard on the right-hand side and the name Assida on the left.

"What the hell is it?" asked Gary.

"It's a money counter," replied Possum.

"A commercial scale and money counter. Why would anyone need those things?" asked Gary sarcastically already knowing the answer.

"To weigh drugs and count money. Drug money," affirmed Possum.

"Of all the cases, down there I chose the one with a scale and cash counter?" asked Sebastian.

"Luck of the draw. But you know that that means? Two things. There's probably all equipment in the rest of those cases. Scales, counters, and other stuff to run a cocaine manufacturing lab in Columbia. My guess is that the main part of the cargo, aka the money, is at six thousand feet inside of the other part of the plane. The light oxidation of the flight cases also means something else. Something more serious," continued Possum.

"What?" asked Sebastian.

"They are gonna be looking for it!"

CHAPTER 7

Everyone welcomed Jules and Rick back on board the ship and were all relieved that she was going to make a full recovery. Rick doted on her and made sure she was comfortable and never without anything she needed. Once they got settled, Rick joined the crew on the deck, and they discussed the salvage.

"I have a question," said Rick.

"Shoot." Replied Possum.

"How many cases do you think are inside of the tail now?"

"Sebastian?"

"I think maybe around fifteen or sixteen."

"I see. Are they all inside the cargo netting?

"Yeah, it's cut open a little on one end but they are still mainly inside."

"Is it that thick yellow two-inch wide ballistic nylon type cargo netting that they use in commercial aviation and shipping?"

"Yeah, I've seen it before in the military in Greece. It's the same stuff all commercial transports use. Super strong."

"That was my next question. So, if it's so strong, then we should be able to hook a much larger lift bag to it and raise them all up at the same time, theoretically."

"Not theoretically, but literally," injected Possum.

"Why don't we use an extra-large lift bag and raise them together then use the ship's crane to put them on the deck. Then we can cover them with a tarp, move quickly to a different location and go through them safely without revealing this location. Like you said, someone is looking for that plane."

"Not someone, but a very dangerous someone," said Possum.

"Any idea who? I can tell from that Possum like grin you know something, Possum," said Rick.

"Indeed, I do. I did some research on that tail number and it's held by a shell company in the Bahamas. I reached out to Carson, our trusty old retired buddy from the FBI and what he told me was quite interesting."

"Go on," said Rick impatiently.

"The company it's owned by is called Island Transport and they are listed as a small island to island moving company. Their revenues are relatively low, yet the company has managed to secure two other cargo planes and several private jets along with large purchases of real estate in the Bahamas and Ft. Lauderdale. That caught the eye of the Bahamian revenue service and the IRS in the states because of the Lauderdale purchase. They bought a massive storage unit business near the airport. It stays full yet turned out to have only one client; Diego Alvarez. He is a suspected kingpin of a large Colombian cartel. Maybe Jules has heard of him. She's from Colombia."

"I'll asked her," said Rick.

"The strangest thing is that their moving company uses up to date Cessna C408 Courier planes inter-island. But they fly a beat up seventy-seven-year-old DC-3 back and forth regularly from the Abacos to Colombia. Why?"

"You tell me," said Rick.

Because DC-3's are the most widely used plane's in central America and they can fly long range with the ability to land on short runways. They are the perfect inconspicuous plane to move drugs and or drug money around."

"What else do you know about this Alvarez guy?" asked Rick.

"Carson told me that he's never been convicted of a major crime and has several top Florida and Colombian lawyers on retainer full-time. He was a person of interest in several murders and is on the radar of the US and Colombia intelligence services. Rumor is that he is ruthless. He was suspected of the beheadings of a rival cartel's drug pin. The man and his entire family were beheaded while on a holiday at their private beach house in Colombia. Fifteen guards were also killed. Not a single person would testify against him and even several of those ended up vanishing after being question by the Colombian authorities. He even killed the two-year-old and four-year-old of the cartel kingpin, Manuel Garcia. Alvarez was never charged."

"Damn he is sadistic if it's true."

Jules stepped onto the deck with a cup of herbal tea and was blowing on it as she walked towards Rick and the crew.

"Hi Jules, we were just talking about you. We think this case and the plane down below might belong to Diego Garcia. Have you heard of him?"

Jules dropped the cup she was holding and it shattered on the deck as she gasped.

"Put it back, put it back! We have to get out of here!" she belted.

Her eyes looked watery and the look of terror was on her face.

"Calm down Jules, no one knows we have this. There are no planes or sea vessels anywhere near here according to the radar," said Rick.

"You don't understand Rick, his nickname is The Butcher. He is untouchable and suspected of hundreds of murders in Colombia. As a young girl he is what Americans think of as the boogie man. He is a modern-day horror character. He likes to behead people and if he catches someone who steals or crosses him he has been known to filet off their skin and wear it as a jacket. He is a psychopathic serial killer. The rumor is that he doesn't kill because he is a drug kingpin. He is a drug kingpin in order to kill. He uses his wealth to murder people for his pleasure. I heard stories that he regularly has hunts on his property near the Parque Nacional Natural Las Hermosas. He has a residence in Palmira."

"So, what, lots of people hunt," said Gary.

"He hunts humans!"

"He owns several rental properties and some hostels. Many young tourists have gone missing from those hostels, and some were found in the park. Many were found fileted like a fish and all of their organs missing. Some people believe he's also selling those on the black market. You have to throw that case overboard now."

Rick put his arm around Jules and patted her on the back.

"I appreciate your input Jules but no one is coming for us here. I promise."

Jules stormed off and gave Rick an ugly look as she disappeared into the main salon. It was the first time ever she was angry like that. It surprised Rick and he followed after her.

"Damn!" said Possum.

"Yeah, she's pissed and scared," said Gary.

"Maybe we should heed her warning," replied Possum.

"We should at least discuss it as a team."

"You're right. I'll get everyone together and have Rick and Jules join us and we can make a decision," said Possum.

RICK AND JULES joined the rest of the crew in the main salon about fifteen minutes after they all sat down. It was obvious that she had been crying.

"Hey guys. We want to make a team decision about this salvage. Is that okay Jules?" asked Gary.

"No! It's not okay! Either put it back or I am leaving the ship. Period!"

"Whoa, whoa, we all kind of thought the same thing. The problem is that the gold is ours and it's in close proximity to the plane. How about we just toss the case over and focus on the gold."

She was whimpering and sobbing and eventually nodded her head in agreement.

"We came here for the gold, not drug money, so let's do what we came here for and get out of here," chimed in Rick.

They all agreed and Rick walked on the deck and threw the case and its contents over the side. He made a motion with his hands that it was over. End of story. He hugged Jules and she was still trembling. Rick gathered his team and the hired crew. Every single person on the ship was in the main salon.

"We are taking some time off and rethinking this salvage. I realize that on a ship it's impossible to keep secrets of what we are salvaging and it's not right anyway. So, from this moment forward, anyone working on this ship has the right to know what's being searched for and hopefully recovered at all times. As for the hired crew from Fort Lauderdale, since I can't make everyone on board a team member and split the bounty so many ways, I have decided to implement a bonus system. If a valuable find is recovered on this salvage or others in the future all hired crew will receive a 10% bonus. We can call it a finder's fee. That way you all feel you have skin in the game. How does that sound?"

They all nodded and some said they were happy with the idea out loud.

"What I need from the crew though is to sign NDA's and nothing, I mean nothing every salvaged or stumbled upon is to be discussed outside of this ship. Do you all understand?"

They all gave a resounding yes together.

"How many of you already know what we pulled up tonight with the ROV?"

He waited and slowly one by one they all raised their hands.

"That's what I thought. What I need you to do now, is forget it ever happened. Don't talk about it, don't text anyone, don't even think about it anymore. Not only is it dangerous but it violates your NDA's and we could fine you and/or even prosecute you for releasing trade secrets."

Gary printed out NDA's and they all signed them. Shortly after Rick thanked the hire crew for their compliance and he and Jules went to their cabin for the night.

THEY COLLECTIVELY DECIDED to bring the ship back to port and regroup. Just being above that plane made them all nervous. The ship got back to the anchorage about midday and Rick gave the hired crew a few days off to relax on Key West. Rick and Jules, along with Gary, Possum and Johnie piled into Rick's Bronco and drove to the Airbnb that they had rented. They would rethink the salvage and try a different way.

Sebastian returned to his condo just off of Mickens Lane, and hit his favorite watering hole that afternoon. The Green Parrot was the scuttlebutt of Key West. It was a short walk for him and he could always stumble home if he had one too many, so he rarely drove there. He sat at his usual barstool and ordered a Heineken. Not long after he was approached by one of his buddies who was also Greek.

He sat down beside him and spoke Greek, something he rarely did. And once the conversation was over, Sebastian quickly paid he tab, ran home and hopped in his old VW Bug and drove straight to the Rick's Airbnb. He was out of breath as he knocked on the door and Johnie opened it.

"Where's Rick. I have to speak to him immediately," he said sounding winded.

Rick heard the commotion and met them in the hallway.

"Come sit down Sebastian, what's going on?" asked Rick

Sebastian sat down at the bar stool in the kitchen and took a few deep breaths.

"Alvarez knows!"

"What?!"

"Garcia Alvarez knows. My Greek buddy said the rumor is all over the island about the sunken plane. He said one of the crew had instant messaged one of his buddies in Key West about what we found and it got around. This island is small. Somehow it got back to Alvarez and he is coming to Key West to find the people who found it. That's us."

"What damn drew member spilled his guts?! I kill him I swear," exclaimed Rick.

"You don't have to. He was found in his apartment today with a Columbian necktie."

Rick put his hand on his forehead and took a deep breath. A Colombian necktie is where a person's throat is cut and their tongue is hung out of the hoe to resemble a necktie.

"He was probably tortured. We have to assume Alvarez's men did this. And if they did, it's only a matter of time before they find us."

"They already have. My friend said they would be contacting us tonight. He wants to make a deal. I'm sure it's a deal we can't refuse."

"Son of a bitch. Jules is gonna lose it," said Rick.

Rick thought for a minute and made a decision.

"Johnie, I want you to take Nine-Tenths back to Destin. Take Chief with you. If I need you to come back, please just board Chief with that nice lady, Suzy Davis. She also has a bird and loves to pet sit. She takes great care of him. She even gave him a shower last time I asked her to pet sit. I'm gonna fly Jules back to Destin and I want her to stay on the boat with you. Keep an eye on her and don't let her go anywhere without you. Pick her up at the airport and keep me posted. Go now."

Johnie didn't hesitate and Gary drove him to Rick's yacht in Stock Island. He was off of the dock in ten minutes, bound for Destin Harbor. Rick tried to slowly relay the news to Jules but she didn't take it well and was a basket case. She protested furiously about going back to Destin. She was scared to be in Key West but also afraid of what could happen to Rick and the boys while she was in Destin. Rick would not take no for an answer and she finally agreed as long as Rick would allow her to pick up her bounty hunting in Destin as long as Johnie accompanied her. He knew there would be no double crossing of Diego Alvarez and he would do whatever he said within reason. All he had to do was wait for him to contact them.

Rick took Jules to the Key West airport and said his tearful goodbyes. Jules hugged him harder than she ever had before.

"You promised to marry me, so don't get yourself killed and break that promise. Okay?"

"I will marry you Jules and soon. Don't worry. This too shall pass," said Rick as he kissed her forehead and she walked to the gate.

She texted him just as the plane taxied down the runway.

He sat in the Bronco and watched as it disappeared into the clouds.

At least she'll be safe in Destin.

Rick drove back to the Airbnb and met Possum at the door.

"Rick, this arrived right after you left. I heard a knock and came to the door and it was sitting here."

It was a shoebox wrapped in newspaper. He sat it on the kitchen table and the team gathered round as he unwrapped it. Inside was a cell phone and note.

Use speed dial one.

Rick put the burner phone on speaker and sat his iPhone beside it and hit record. He pushed speed dial one.

"Hola, Rick Waters. I am the owner of what you discovered. We need to meet."

"When and where?"

"Ocho at El Meson De Pepe's, asked for Juan. Come alone."

He hung up and that was that.

"Now what?" asked Gary.

"I guess I'm going to a Cuban restaurant tonight."

Rick shared the recording to Possum using Airdrop. He pulled it into Studio One and grabbed some headphones to see if he could make out any of the background sounds to find a possible location of the phone. He sent the number to Carson and he would get the cell info and try to locate the closest cell tower it pinged off of. Rick let Possum do his magic and paced in the kitchen anxious about his meeting.

"What do you think he will ask?" asked Gary.

"I think he's going to demand, not ask us to salvage the contents of the plane crash and give it to him. I have a counter offer. There's no way we can refuse. He will just have us all assassinated."

"Won't he just do it after we give up the goods?"

"To the victor go the spoils," said Rick with a grin.

"Double cross?"

"Not exactly, I'll explain after I meet with him."

RICK PARKED the Bronco on Green Street and moseyed towards the restaurant. It was busy as usual. It had one of the best locations for dinner on the island sitting at the entrance to Mallory Square. A Cuban band was blasting salsa out front as he told the hostess he was meeting Juan who was already seated. She had him follow her and they went through the kitchen to a hidden room in the back. She gave a special knock at the door and a large Colombian man opened the door and let Rick inside. He frisked him and motioned for him to sit at a table in the corner of the room. A few minutes later a man with a dark beard and receding hairline walked through a back door and walked towards Rick.

"Rick Waters, I am Juan Esteban. I will be your liaison."

"Where's Diego."

Juan looked surprised when Rick said his name.

"I know no Diego. I represent a group from Colombia who has interest in something you have stumbled across."

"Cut the bullshit Juan. I know the cargo plane belongs to Diego Alvarez and is full of drug money and paraphernalia. Now let's be gentlemen and get down to business."

"Very well. I like your candor. From now on his name will not be spoken and he will be referred to as Jefe, fair?"

"Fair."

"Jefe demands that you retrieve what is his and he will not make an effort to stop you or attack anyone involved now or after."

"I have a counteroffer. Tell Jefe, I will retrieve what belongs to him for a ten percent finder's fee plus expenses. Otherwise, he will never see it again. Fair?"

It was obvious that Juan was offended by his counteroffer but he thought for moment, then spoke.

"I will relay your offer to Jefe and call you on the phone with his response."

They shook hands and Rick walked out of the meeting. He realized his hands were trembling a little. He had just made a demand to one of the most dangerous men in the world. He needed a beer to calm his nerves but chose to stay sober and just try and relax. He and Jules had never discussed if they would now drink since she found out she wasn't pregnant but he was feeling so good after his dry out time, he decided to keep going. He was thinking clearly and sleeping better. There was no sense in ruining a good thing. If anytime in his life he needed a clear head, it was now.

Once back at the Airbnb he relayed the info to the team.

"So, what now?" asked Gary.

"We wait," said Rick.

JULES ARRIVED SAFELY in Destin and Johnie picked her up as planned. She and Rick talked and he told her it was all gonna work out fine. She wasn't convinced but knew that he didn't have much of a choice now that Alvarez knew they had found the plane. She just implored him to be careful which he agreed. She told Rick she was going to try and stay busy and take few easy bail jump cases along with Johnie and split the reward with him. She needed to get her mind off of the danger Rick and the boys might be facing. It wasn't long after Rick hung up with Jules that the burner phone rang. He picked it up but forgot to record it and put it on speaker. It didn't matter. It was short and sweet.

"Go ahead, this is Rick."

"We accept your offer. Begin now."

Juan hung up and Rick called a meeting.

"I have let the hired crew go and we will continue opera-tions without them. It's far too dangerous for hired crew to be on this mission. We won't be traveling far on the ship and with..."

He started counting on his fingers.

"With five of us, including Sebastian, we can run the ship and carry out the salvage. Anything from the recording?"

"Listen to this," said Possum as he handed Rick the headphones.

He shut his eyes and listened. The conversation with Juan was clear and clean and he backed it up and tried to ignore what they were saying and listened to the background sounds. He backed it up a few times and then he heard it.

It was a sound he had heard before. Far in the background he heard a over a speaker, 'Daffy Duck, your order is ready'. It was the outside speaker at the Keys Fisheries in Marathon. As far as he knew they were the only restaurant in the Key that used cartoon characters names for the waitlist for a table. Hell, he and Jules had just eaten there. It was a lucky break.

"They are on a boat in the marina next to Keys Fisheries. They have to be. We need to case the place. Did you hear back from Carson yet?"

"Not but I'll call him again. Why don't you hit speed dial again and see if you can keep him on the phone longer and I'll record it."

This time Possum put a suction cup recording device to the back of the burner phone. Rick pushed the number.

"Juan, I hate to bother you but we need supplies. We

can't start until tomorrow. We need provisions and more lift bags and other tools. Can you let Jefe know?"

"Hold on."

He put his hand over the receiver as Rick waited.

"Jefe is not happy but understands. You can begin tomorrow."

Rick hung up the phone and Possum downloaded the recording into his DAW (Digital Audio Workstation). After adjusting the EQ for voice, he heard it again.

"Roadrunner, your order is ready."

Now they were certain. He also heard someone in the background talking to Jefe but only hearing one side of the conversation. He knew that Jefe aka Diego Garcia was not there and they were speaking to him on a phone. He was most likely in Colombia.

CHAPTER 8

Gary and Possum ran to Miami to pick up salvage supplies while Rick took the Bronco to Marathon. He had already met Juan and needed a cover; so, he donned a beard, a beach hat, sunglasses and binoculars. To complete his ensemble, he wore a t-shirt that had a flying logo that read Bird Nerd. He also borrowed Possum's Canon 80D with his longest lens. He drove to the to the north side of Key's Fisheries and hid his Bronco behind a building. He went to the water's edge and took photos of birds and tried to act like he was not interested in the goings on in the marina. With one eye on birds and the other on the Marina he tried to spot Juan. The nicest boat in the Marina was a cigarette boat named "Necisito".

How obvious!

He found a pile of old lobster traps and flipped over a five-gallon bucket and placed the Canon under some palm fronds pointed at the speedboat. Stakeouts were boring but he was prepared and brought a sandwich and his RTIC cooler backpack with some waters inside. He had Possums bird guide book and occasionally glanced at it as he kept an eye on the marina. About two hours into this stake some men came up to the deck from down below. He immediately started snapping photos of them using the auto settings. He was ducked down so they couldn't see him but the left in a dark colored SUV.

Once they were out of sight, he picked up the camera and reviewed the photos. As he zoomed in, he recognized one of them. It was Juan and he had left with two other men in the SUV. He hopped in the Bronco and drove to the other side then walked down the dock. He had his lock-picking bag tucked under his shirt in the rear waistband of his hiking shorts. He strolled down the dock pretending to be looking for a lost dog in case there were still men on the cigarette boat. He had to work fast.

"Scruffy, Scruffy, where are you boy?"

He whistled a few times then yelled it louder standing directly behind the stern of the cigarette boat.

"Scruffy, come here boy."

The dock was barren. He quickly climbed onto fast boat and picked the lock. Once inside he removed one of the plastic ceiling light covers and installed a listening device. It screwed right into the light socket, and the bulb screwed into it. It was completely inconspicuous and would never run out of batteries. It would transmit about two hundred yards to a sending unit he hid by the lobster traps that went to a voicemail recorder. Now any conversations onboard would be recorded and they could get the jump on the cartel. The sending unit had a three-day rechargeable battery life, so he added a small solar panel that would keep the batteries topped off. As long as no one stumbled upon it, it would be fine where it was. In case someone did find it, he put a danger high voltage sticker on it and hoped that would keep even the nosiest person from messing with it. He returned to Key West and waited for Gary and Possum to return.

Sebastian took his own personal dinghy out to the ship on anchor and waited for a text from Rick. He would transport them to the ship with the supplies once they were ready.

It was 6:30 pm when Gary and Possum got back from Miami.

"Mission was a success! Possum, can Carson still put together a team from the FBI? I know he's retired but he still has a lot of pull there doesn't he? Can you call him. I'd like to put a special investigative team together and have them stay at my place. Now that I have planted the listening device in the boat, we just need a translator," said Possum.

"How about Jules?"

"You freaking genius. Jules will be safer with a team of FBI agents around her and she will also still be involved. That'll kill two birds with one stone. No pun intended," said Rick, as he pointed at his *Bird Nerd* shirt.

"I'll call him now,' said Possum.

"Can you put him on speaker. It's been a while since I've spoken to him?"

"No problem amigo."

"Hey Carson, it's Possum with Rick and the team. I'm gonna put you on speaker, okay?"

"Hey guys. How's everyone?"

"We're great Carson. But we need a favor from ya. Possum, go ahead."

"Carson, we need your help. I know you still have some pull down at the FBI. Do you think you can put together a small task force to go down to Destin and help with some reconnaissance and keep an eye on Jules. Remember when I told you we got mixed up with a bad dude from Colombia when we accidentally found his sunken cargo plane?"

"How could I forget?"

"Well, it's gotten worse. He got wind that we found it and is forcing us to recover it and turn it over to him. Rick sent Jules up to Destin to be safe. She's terrified of this guy as she should be. Rick managed to hide a listening device on one of the fast boats that is used by Alvarez's guy who is our contact to him. They'll be speaking in Spanish and probably some codes. Jules can translate the Spanish if your team can handle to codes."

"I may be retired but they still use me on occasion on contract. They will be more than interested to get Alvarez. He has avoided being convicted over a dozen times. If we can get him on something bug and put him away, it would be a big win for the US. He mainly had dealt cocaine in the past, but the street talk is that he has moved to Fentanyl and it's killing a lot of people. I'd love to bust that son of a bitch. Count me in."

"Carson, it's Gary, why don't you and your team stay in my condo. It sleeps six comfortably."

"Oh yeah, I remember your bachelor mansion. If it's not an imposition, that would be great."

"No imposition whatsoever, I'll be here and it's empty. Jules has an extra key. Johnie will be staying with her at her and Rick's place to keep an eye on her. You never know what Alvarez is capable of, so we wanted to take her out of the equation."

"Alright, sounds like a plan. I'll put together the guys and make contact when we are about to head down there."

"Thanks Carson. Talk soon."

They all chimed in their goodbye and Possum disconnected. Rick started to feel a little better about Jules being up in Destin. With not only Johnie protecting her, but a team of FBI agents two doors down, he felt she would be safe.

"There's no sense in salvaging under the cover of darkness now. The true owners of the plan know we are here. We may as well start. You ready Sebastian?"

He stretched out his hands and gave a nod. Rick and Gary lowered the ROV into the water with the crane. Once it was in the water, Sebastian began the dive. He had preset GPS coordinates that would put the ROV just behind the tail. Once in place he slowly motored inside. They all crowded around the video screen. As he moved forward the bright yellow cargo net came into focus. Just as Sebastian had said, it was cut open. But if he could hook the lift bag to the bottom and top part of the cargo net then it should lift it up like a sack and all the cases should stay inside. He used the thruster to get into position. The nylon lift bag line was affixed to large D-rings. All he had to do was push them against the stiff cargo net and secure them. Before the dive they had replaced the cutting arm with another gripping arm and attached D-rings to each end. Once they were pushed into place and snapped over the netting all he had to do was release the D-ring and it would be hooked to the net. He did the lowest one first as it was more difficult than the top. He pushed against the net but there wasn't enough resistance to open the D-ring. It gave him an idea. He switched tactics and did the top first. It was taut and slipped onto the net easily. Once secured he moved back into place and used his grabbing arm to pull against the bottom of the net. Then, with the right arm slide the D-ring on secure. It worked.

They he moved up a little higher towards the middle and hooked both grabbing arms to the cargo net. He used his reverse thrusters. The bag wasn't moving. He gave it full throttle and it only budged a little. It just wasn't going to come out.

"How long does the lift bag take to fill?" asked Rick.

"I believe the large one will take about thirty seconds to fully inflate," replied Possum.

"But even partially inflated it will begin to lift, right?"

"Yeah, it should."

"Sebastian, what you need to do. Never mind, it's too hard to explain. Just hand me the controller."

Sebastian handed over the joystick to Rick and he backed the ROV outside of the opening of the plane and hit the release button that dropped the lift bag that was attached to the hull. It slowly sank down until the line was taut and slightly pulling on the cargo netting. With one of the grabbing arms, he snagged the nylon lift bag line and moved it to the far-right side of the plane and moved the ROV to the left side and grabbed the net with both arms.

"Sebastian, I need your hands here. I'm going to use the reverse thrusters to pull against the net and I need you to hit the fill button for the lift bag. When it's about halfway inflated, it will begin pulling against the net at the same time as I am using full reverse thrust. It should be enough to pull it to the end of the tail section. The trick is we must time it perfectly. So, when I say now, push both buttons to release the grabber arms and I should rocket backwards out of the plane just as the bag hits full lift. You understand?"

"Got it!"

Rick took a deep breath and began to pull on the cargo netting with the reverse thrusters.

"Go ahead and fill the bag,"

Sebastian used his thumb to push the fill button on the side of the controller Rick was holding with both hands. In the screen they all could see the nylon line rise to the top right side of the plan and begin to pull the net. As the lift bag inflated the cargo began to move. Rick was counting out loud as it continued to move.

"twenty-four, twenty-five, now!"

Sebastian pushed both buttons to release the gripper arms it began to move away from the tail, then a cloud of sediment blocked out the screen. It went black.

"I've lost control. Look!"

The depth gauge of the ROV began to go higher. The screen was still black as it sank. Two hundred, three hundred, four hundred, it just kept sinking.

"What the hell is going on?"

"Look Rick," yelled Gary as he pointed off the port side of the ship.

The bright yellow bag had broken the surface. Gary and Possum jumped into the inflatable and motored over to it as fast as they could. Possum secured the lift bag to the side of the dinghy and towed it next to the ship. Once in position

Sebastian lowered the crane down and Possum hooked it to the bottom of the lift bag then deflated it. He slowly and meticulously lifted it out of the water and sat it on the middle of the deck of the ship. Rick just stared at the ROV control arm screen. It just kept going deeper. It finally stopped falling after thirty minutes and settled at sixty-six hundred feet. Rick assumed when he lost control that it dove to the bottom of the shelf and sat on the sea floor. The screen was still washed out but ever so slowly an image began to emerge. It was upside down.

Rick turned his head then flipped the controller upside down as the image became clearer. The ROV was tangled with some of the tails wiring that was dangling from the ripped open tail.

"Can you back it out?" asked Possum.

"I'll try."

Rick used the thrusters to try reverse. It didn't move, so he tried forward and it moved forward about a foot and then stopped. It was stuck and stuck good.

"Can you spin it around? Use forward and reverse," interjected Gary.

Rick used full throttle and spun the ROV around. It still would not release from the cable but off in the distance, they saw it. It was the other half of the DC-3 lying upside down on the dark ocean floor. The ROV was caught on cables that protruded from the bottom of the DC-3 tail section. So based on the video image coming from the ROV, both parts of the plane were now settled upside own at sixty-six hundred feet.

"The ROV is lost. There's no way to dislodge it from the cables of the tail. Can you order another one? Also, how much battery life does it have?" asked Rick.

Gary ran into the salon to call the manufacturer of the ROV as Sebastian read through the owner's manual of the ROV. It says 72 hours on standby. Rick immediately turned off the lights and cameras of the ROV and brought it down to standby.

"We need an ROV to raise the plane. If we can get another ROV, then we can retrieve this ROV. We can either sell one of them or keep them both. It's just a same to lose one and all that money. We need at least one to get the contents of the plane up at that depth."

A few minutes later, Gary rejoined the crew on the deck.

"I have bad news. The manufacture says they are three months behind schedule on orders. I offered to pay him double, and he said he would move us to the front of the line, but it would still take a month. I called two more companies that make ROV's, and they don't have anything that can handle that depth."

"We're screwed," said Rick.

"Maybe not," said Possum.

"We have the two-man sub."

"Are you nuts? That thing is only rated to five-thousand

feet. It's still another sixteen hundred feet to the plane. Plus, we will be inside of it!"

"Hear me out. These things are rated at certain depths for liability. They can handle far more pressure than they are rated for. Like maybe one third more. Sixteen hundred feet more shouldn't even get close to its max depth possibility."

"I hear what you are saying but two of us will be inside. That is a huge danger. We must think of something else."

"We could fish for it?" exclaimed Sebastian.

"Fish for it?" asked Rick.

"Yeah, I've seen these videos on YouTube where people throw magnets and pull up metal objects from rivers and streams. If we could get a big enough magnet, we could raise it with a winch."

"That's a great idea Sebastian and really thinking outside of the box. There's just one problem. The plane is aluminum. Magnets won't work," said Rick.

"Dammit, that's right! What was I thinking?"

"I'll contact Juan and tell him what we have so far and say we need more time. That's all we can do. Possum you can record this end and the listening device will record the other end. Then we can sync them and forward it to Carson's team."

They all gathered in the main salon after the team opened all the cases and took inventory. It was all drug gear. More scales and a curious amount of filtration masks, gloves and laboratory equipment like flasks, mixers, and other lab equipment. It appeared that Alvarez was planning on doing his own manufacturing and breaking away from China, who was probably his main supplier. He was already making buckets of money moving the deadly drug, but greed made him want even more.

Rick would try and get as much evidence on tape as he could to entrap Alvarez. He dialed the number as Possum hit record on his field recorder.

"Hola."

"Hi Juan, it's Rick Waters. We managed to get the contents of the tail section for Diego Alvarez, I mean Jefe."

"Be discreet Waters. I told you."

"My apologies. We have secured fifteen flight cases with drug scales and laboratory equipment. No cash yet. It's still in the other section of the DC-3 but we've run into a problem."

"Look, I know what was on the plane down to the last detail. I don't need a rundown on the phone. What is the problem?"

"We lost our ROV and need to order another one. We need a month to get a new one."

"Out of the question. I will call Jefe. He will not be pleased."

Juan hung up.

"He doesn't sound happy," said Possum.

"Yeah, but he just verified who Jefe is. That's all I really wanted out of that call. They are gonna call back with a demand we get it sooner."

Just as Rick predicted, Juan called back.

"Jefe says you have a week. He wants to see what you have recovered already and have it delivered to East Bahia Honda Key tomorrow. There is a flat area on the north side where you can land a helicopter. Bring the cases and be there at 11:00pm. I will arrive later and retrieve them."

Juan hung up again before Rick could speak.

"I have an idea. Do you think you can borrow a boat from Big Pine Key?" asked Rick to Sebastian.

"Borrow? Umm, yeah sort of, what size. Just an inflatable or something. Anything to get us out to East Bahia Honda Key before the drop. Possum do you still have those camouflaged motion cameras you wanted to use to video some Key Deer?"

"Yeah, they are in my travel bag. I have three of them."

"Okay, let's go place them on the island before we make the drop," said Rick.

They took Sebastian's dinghy back to Key West and climbed into Rick's Bronco. Once they got to Big Pine Key, Rick dropped off Sebastian at Sunshine RV Park and drove over to the visitor center. They parked, walked around the back, and made their way to the bank near the mangroves and waited. Within ten minutes they hear the whine of the outboard motor approaching. They quickly climbed in and Sebastian motored fast towards the little remote island. They waded over and Possum set up the three cameras on small shrub trees that surrounded the flat area they planned to land the chopper at the next night. They motored back to Big Pine Key and Rick picked up Sebastian on A1A. No one even knew he borrowed a dinghy tied up on the dock wall inside the little marina. They drove back to Key West then returned to the ship. It was time to attempt a dive in the sub.

"So, what are we doing? Drawing straws?"

"No, it's too dangerous. I will go and anyone who is not comfortable just say so. I need one volunteer."

"I'll go with you, hombre. We've been running together for a long time. What's one more adventure. Right?" said Possum with a little chuckle.

Although he was making light of it to ease the tension. He knew fully well how dangerous it was. Gary and Sebastian hooked up the sub to the crane and Rick and Possum climbed in. It was not as tight inside as Rick imagined and it was built like a tank but if anything at all failed on the sub it would be disaster.

Rick and Possum looked out of the large super thick spherical glass of the front of the sub as it was lowered into the water from the deck of their research vessel. Their mission was clear—a trial run to see how the sub reacted. The small two-man submersible, appropriately named the Deep Blue, was their ticket to unraveling the mysteries that lay beneath the surface. But little did they know that their journey would soon turn into a battle against the crushing depths and their own fears. Rick was up for the adventure, and Possum, a brilliant researcher were a perfect team. Their shared passion for the unknown fueled their determination to push boundaries. Today, however, they were about to test the limits of the submersible and their own courage.

"Are you sure about this, Possum?" Rick asked, his voice filled with a mix of excitement and apprehension.

Possum glanced at Rick, his eyes betraying a hint of doubt. "I've done the calculations, Rick. The sub should be able to withstand the pressure at sixty-six hundred feet. But I can't guarantee it'll be a smooth ride."

Rick nodded, a bead of sweat trickling down his forehead. The tension between them was palpable as they prepared for their descent. Deep Blue, a sleek metallic vessel, seemed both sturdy and fragile against the vastness of the ocean.

As they descended into the depths, the light from the surface faded leaving them in an inky blackness punctuated only by the sub's dimly lit control panel. The pressure mounted with each passing minute, weighing on their minds and bodies.

"Possum, are you sure we can handle this?" Rick's voice trembled with uncertainty. The sub creaked and groaned under the increasing weight, amplifying his unease.

Possum swallowed hard, his hands gripping the controls tightly. "We've prepared for this, Rick. Deep Blue's hull is reinforced with advanced materials. But there are no guarantees when we venture into uncharted territory."

Minutes stretched into hours as they descended further into the abyss. They were taking the decent slow. The pressure gauge crept higher and higher, while the eerie silence of the deep surrounded them. Their only solace was the steady hum of the sub's occasional off gasses, a fragile thread connecting them to the surface world. Suddenly, a low rumble reverberated through the hull, sending a shiver down their spines. The sub shook violently, and panic gripped their hearts. Rick's mind raced with thoughts of impending doom, his worst fears manifesting before him. They had reached fifty-eight hundred feet; eight hundred feet more than the sub was rated for.

"Possum! What's happening?" Rick shouted; his voice strained with fear.

"I don't know, Rick!" Possum shouted back, his eyes wide with alarm. "Hold on tight! We need to stabilize the sub!"

With trembling hands, they fought against the chaos that threatened to consume them. Deep Blue groaned under the immense pressure, its outer shell protesting against the forces at play. It was a terrifying dance with fate, as they battled to keep their fragile vessel intact.

Time seemed to lose all meaning as they fought for survival in the depths of the ocean. The sub's systems flickered, warning lights flashing, and the control panel displayed a cascade of critical errors. Yet, they persisted, their determination unwavering, despite the overwhelming odds stacked against them.

"It's a built-in safety warning. Hang on, let me override it. It's designed to keep idiots like us from going beyond the factory rating," said Possum.

Just when they thought they couldn't hold on any longer, the tumultuous shaking ceased. The submersible stabilized, its battered exterior a testament to the trials of the pressure. They exchanged glances, their faces etched with both relief and a newfound respect for the unforgiving power of the ocean. The sub gently sat down on the ocean floor, only a few yards from the DC-3's main fuselage.

Rick let out a shaky breath, his body trembling from the lingering adrenaline. "Possum... We made it."

Possum managed a weak smile, his voice barely a whisper. "So far, so good."

They focused the subs lights on the plane and could see similar cargo netting peeking from the broken frame of the plane.

"What do you think our best bet is?" asked Rick.

"I think we should try and free the ROV from the tail and use it. I have no desire to return down here again."

"Yeah, let's do it."

They lifted up a foot and hovered just off the bottom of the sea floor. Possum had the video recorders running since they broke the surface. He slowly and deliberately used the thrusters to get closer to the trapped ROV. When it came into view Rick could see that the left landing skeg was wrapped up in some hydraulic hose.

"We have to cut it loose."

Deep Blue had similar cutting and grabbing arms as the ROV. Possum positioned the little sub right in front of it closer to Ricks cutting arm side on the port side. He extended the little arm out towards the ROV and tried to snap the hydraulic hose. It wasn't cutting. It kept folding over sideways when he tried to cut it.

"Just cut the edge of it. I have an idea," said Possum.

Rick pulled the arm back a little and positioned the cutting on the edge of the hose with the pointed part of the snips. He squeezed them and it cut a little of the hose as hydraulic fluid began to seep from it. Possum grabbed the right skeg with the grabber arm on the starboard side and pulled in full reverse. The ROV popped loose and flew towards the two-man sub smashing into the front spherical glass window. They both held their breath. No cracks.

Rick let out a huge breath.

"Contact Gary on the surface to raise the ROV."

"Fuck that! Let's take it with us. I've got a great grip on it and we can just ascend. Let's get the hell out of here before we end up tiny little pieces all over the ocean floor."

Together they began the slow ascent toward the surface, leaving behind the depths that had tested their limits. The tension that had gripped them now transformed into a deep sense of accomplishment and a profound appreciation for the fragility of life.

As the Deep Blue breached the surface, sunlight flooded the cabin bathing them in its warmth. They emerged from the depths forever changed—heroes who had dared to venture beyond what was known, facing their fears head-on and emerging triumphant and more importantly, alive.

CHAPTER 9

O nce the ROV and the Deep Blue were secured back on the deck, Rick disappeared into this cabin and called Jules. He explained to her that everything was on schedule and didn't mention his trip down in the deep waters. She would be upset and had already enough on her mind. With the ROV back in service, he had no desire to ever go that deep again.

"I'm glad everything is going as planned Rick. Carson called me. Johnie and I are picking them up from the Destin airport tonight. I'm gonna give Carson the keys to my Bronco and I'll just ride with Johnie on a little easy case tomorrow. It's not dangerous. It's a woman who was charged with a domestic. She didn't show for court, so I gotta bring her in. She's smaller than me and other than the alleged domestic she has no criminal record. Don't worry, Johnie will be with me the entire time."

"Okay Jules. Just be careful."

"I will I promise. You do the same."

"Always baby. Talk soon."

They hung up and met Possum in the main salon with Capt. Lane and Gary.

"So, what's the plan?"

"I've been watching the video we shot on our dive. The way the plane is sitting, I think we should just raise the entire plane at once instead of trying to go inside and pull out the cargo. There is a chance we could get the ROV hung up again. I don't think either of us wants to go back down in that sub to break it loose again. Do you?"

"You make valid point there, Possum."

"Look at the edge where the tail broke off from the main fuselage," said Possum as he pointed to the video screen.

"I'm looking," replied Rick.

"If we hook the lift bags there on three even distances apart, we can lift the plane up off the bottom, then it will rise with the nose pointing down and when it arrives on the surface we can use scuba to remove the cargo bags out separately with smaller lift bags as a safe depth. Once we have all the cargo out, we can just release the plane, and let it sink down to its watery grave forever."

"I like it, I like it a lot," said Rick in the voice of Jim Carrey as he often did.

Possum nodded in agreement with a big grin on his face.

"If we can send the ROV down and take video after the plane is empty, we may be able to fool Alvarez that it was already picked clean. I don't know if he'll buy it and I'm not sure I wanna do that, but I think under the circumstances we need all the options we can get," added Rick.

"We are going to need some massive lift bags to raise that plane," said Gary.

"I wouldn't say massive but yes, larger. The weight to water aspect ratio is much different than weight on land. When immersed up to the level of your chest to neck, buoyancy lessens the impact of gravity resulting in a significant reduction of your body weight. For instance, someone weighing two hundred pounds on land would weigh approximately less than forty pounds in water that reaches their neck. This demonstrates a decrease of about 75-90% in weight due to buoyancy," said Possum.

"Well thank you, Archimedes," said Rick.

"My pleasure, Linus Pauling," replied Possum.

"Okay, I'll have to look that one up. I'm sure it's a diss of some sort."

"Yeah, he was the chemist who got the model for DNA completely wrong."

"That's a stretch," said Rick with a laugh.

"It works. I couldn't think of any famous mathematicians who got things dead wrong, but he was close. A bit of a reach, maybe."

"So where are we going to get lift bags big enough to lift three quarters of a DC-3 full of cargo to the surface?" asked Rick.

"The US Coast Guard, naturally," said Possum.

"They aren't just gonna let us borrow them," said Rick.

"Nope, but if they don't know it's missing, they won't be looking for it. We just need a Trojan horse."

Possum devised a plan to meet with the Coast Guard and bring in an old Cuban boat on a flat bed and have Sebastian hide inside. He had seen one lying on its sides in the mangroves. It was crusty and looked like it had been there for some time. Homemade rafts and boats were a common occurrence in the Keys and with Key West being only ninety miles from Cuba. They often ended up here.

"If we can put it on a flatbed trailer and cover up Sebastian with some old tarps and oyster bags, we can distract them and he can slip out and secure the lift bags. We just need a uniform, and we can get that at the Army Navy surplus. I saw lift bags and other salvage operation gear in building seven. It's not far from the main gate. All we need is a distraction and dolly and we are in business."

RICK, Gary and Possum spent the afternoon pulling the old busted Cuban boat onto a flatbed they had rented, as Sebastian went uniform shopping. Once the boat was tied down to the flatbed, Gary returned to the Airbnb to wait. Gary and Possum met Sebastian on Trumbo Road a few blocks from the Coast Guard station. Rick hid a hand truck inside the boat and covered Sebastian with an old tarp and threw in some mangrove branches for good measure. When they approached the main gate pulling the beat-up Cuban boat, they were stopped and questioned.

"What's your business?" asked the guard.

"We are here to see Chief Petty Officer Higgins. He did the initial inspection of my fifty-five-foot Viking that your station helped tow in."

"Oh yeah, I remember that. What's with the old tub?"

"Well, we found it and search it. There were some soggy Cuban cigars on board but no souls. I wasn't sure what the protocol was about disposing of it. Since I needed to get some paperwork about the tow, I need to take to my insurance agent, I thought I'd swing by here and kill two birds with one stone. I figured ya'll would tell me what to do with it. Impound it or just take it to the dump," explained Rick.

"You can just take it to the dump. We don't want it here. I'll need to search it before you park."

"Is Officer Higgins office in that building?" asked Rick as he pointed behind the guard.

He instinctively turned around and Sebastian climbed out and motioned to the guard that he'd search it. He must've assumed Sebastian had just approached the boat from behind.

"I'll take care of it," said Sebastian as she climbed back in the old boat and pulled up the tap and pretend to search.

The guard gave a head nod and seemed uninterested.

"You can park right over there by that building. Officer Higgins is in building eight. You'll need these passes."

The guard took down their names and ID's and gave them badges to hang on their shirts. Gary and Possum parked the rented truck and flat-bed and proceeded to building eight. Sebastian took the hand truck when the coast was clear to building seven. Coast Guard personnel were everywhere; all doing their daily duties. He fit right in and went unabated to the supply area. It was an open area and once he located the lift bags, he pulled down the boxes and stacked them on the hand truck. He strolled out without checking them out with anyone and was never even noticed. He pushed the cart between the building and the old Cuban boat and loaded them inside making sure he wasn't seen. Once it was loaded, he climbed in and covered himself up. Rick and Possum returned a few minutes later after wasting time in building eight. They never met with anyone. They returned their badges to the gate guard and proceeded right out of the Coast Guard station.

They drove straight back to the area they had found the Cuban boat and dumped it back where they had found it in the first place. They dropped off the lift bags at Rick's Airbnb and Sebastian returned the rental truck and trailer. Once they all returned to the ship the sun was low in the sky.

Soon they would make their attempt to raise the crashed DC-3.

The skeleton crew readied the ship for the trip out to the salvage site. Possum threw together a high carb meal of jerk chicken pasta to give them all energy. Once at the site, they secured the anchor and dropped the ROV overboard with two quick release heavy lift bags in tow. They would need two trips down to the sunken plane as the ROV only had two arms and they needed three bags secured to the fuselage in equal distances apart.

Sebastian guided the ROV carefully down. It took over four hours to secure the bags into place using industrial D-rings. It was 9:00 by the time the ROV resurfaced. While Sebastian was securing the D-rings; Rick, Possum and Gary took a complete inventory of the contents of the flight cases recovered from the tail section. Possum took photos of each item he planned to share with the FBI. Once it was all logged and photographed, the loaded it on the helicopter. They had to remove the rear seats to make room for the cases, so only two people could take the flight to the little island where they would make the drop. It would be Sebastian and Rick. They lifted off at 9:20pm and flew towards Big Pine Key. One they cleared Key West airspace they were in the clear to the little island. He called Juan and told him the property recovered from the tail section was ready for pick up on the little key.

Sebastian gently touched down and one by one they

stacked the cases on the broken coral-based clearing. Rick made sure to mention in conversation to Sebastian that they knew they were being filmed and doing this with the FBI's knowledge. The last thing they wanted to do was be criminally involved with smuggling lab gear for a Fentanyl drug lab. The motion detection cameras would catch and record their entire operation. They were off the island and bound back to the ship by 11:26pm. They would have to work late into the night to get the fuselage to the surface.

With the third lift bag in place, Sebastian initiated the remote filling of the bags. It was quite a clever design that Possum came up with. In order to fill the bags a cord would have to be pulled to release gas from the extra-large CO_2 canisters. They were connected to some nylon cords. Possum secured some heavy-duty balloons to the cords and they were all floating above the plane close to each other. All Sebastian had to do was grip them with the grabber arm of the ROV and use his reverse thrusters to engage the bags. He pulled them and immediately the huge lift bags began to fill. He backed away a safe distance and aimed the ROV at the bags and plane. As they watched the bags grew larger and began to pull against the plane. Possum was holding his finger crossed as he watched. The plane began to lift slowly off the ocean floor. It creaked and groaned in the speaker as it lifted sending sediment sideways. It slowly began to tilt to its side and the starboard wing lay on the surface. It rotated a little as it lifted and soon both wings were free from the bottom. The only thing touching was the nose. As the bag lifted, they began to expand and soon the plane dangled a few feet off the murky bottom. After a few minutes it was complete inverted as if it was taking a dive straight down, nose first. As slow as molasses it began to rise. Rick watched the depth; within five minutes it broke the five-thousand-foot mark. It took over forty-five minutes to get within a hundred feet.

With scuba gear loaded onto the inflatable, Rick and Gary motored over the area the plane lift bags would surface. Once it broke the surface, they secured the bags with a tow line and dragged it close to the ship. They donned their scuba gear using full-face masks with radio communication capabilities. Rick pulled a stainless-steel winch cable with him as he descended. Gary had dual flood lights and as Rick hovered over the giant opening of the plane; Rick dove inside and securer the first cargo net. They were lashed to the inside of the plane's fuselage with tie downs, so Rick had to remove each one individually. The entrance to the plane floated about thirty feet below the surface, so they had no worries about getting bent. They could work continuously and just change tanks when needed. It was a joint operation. Sebastian, P-Roy and Possum handled the crane and stacking of the cases while Gary and Rick took turns diving inside the plane and shackling the cargo net to the stainless-steel lift cable.

About five hours into the operation, the final cargo bag was removed and placed on the deck. Gary kicked to the middle of the area that secured the plane to the lift bags and Rick gave him a motion to cut the cords. Gary reached inside his left calf and pulled out his dive knife. He sawed through the cords and the plane began to sink slowly at first, once he cut the last cord it rocketed downwards, the remaining lift bag ling swirling behind it. Gary moved away but suddenly one of the cords caught the back of his scuba tank and began to pull him downwards. He was plummeting to the ocean depths. He desperately tried to free himself from the nylon line. Rick saw what was happening and kicked down towards Gary with every bit of energy he could muster. He caught up with him at about sixty feet. He grabbed ahold of his buoyancy compensator and pulled at the cord. They were now below a hundred feet and descending rapidly. They both continued to struggle with the line. The weight of the plane was pulling them down so fast he was afraid they would be taken down to their deaths. As they approached a hundred and fifty feet and passed the edge of the shelf the sound of the water in their ears felt heavy. Rick sawed at the cord with his knife and it finally twisted and broke free. Rick looked down at his depth gauge and they were at a hundred and seventy-five feet.

They both had about a half a tank of air and slowly ascended to sixty feet and held for a few minutes. They then rose to forty feet and held for ten minutes. Once they got to thirty, they held for another ten minutes then hovered at about twenty feet unit their tanks got to the red zone. Rick was confident they wouldn't get bent but had Sebastian ready the chopper in case they needed to be airlifted to a recompression chamber. Doing the long safety stops while ascending was the smartest thing they could do. Once back on board the ship, they removed their gear and rested in the salon.

Possum counted forty flight cases on board and another hundred and fifty heavily wrapped waterproof bags. After catching their breath, Rick donned a respirator and put on the bags on the work bench. He asked everyone to leave the area in case it was Fentanyl or some other toxic substance. Since he had an idea that Alvarez would be manufacturing Fentanyl in Colombia, he wasn't too concerned but didn't want to take any chances.

As he carefully sliced through the bag and pulled it apart, he saw what he was expecting in the first place, cash. Twenty-dollar bills in two-thousand-dollar bundles wrapped purple and white bands. He pulled them all out and counted them. There were two hundred stacks in the bag. He quickly did the math in his head, and it added up to four hundred thousand dollars. Multiplied by a hundred and fifty bags, the total would be roughly sixty million dollars. He assumed all the bags were cash, that would be why Diego Alvarez was so demanding they retrieve his plane's contents. Rick had every intention of returning fifty million dollars to the island. He planned to keep ten million for his efforts. He knew Alvarez would never pay him a finder's fee and since he had a massive head start on the salvage they hid all the stash in the holds below the ship.

Rick contacted Carson to see if there were any developments from the listening device, he had planted on Juans fast boat.

"Hi Rick. I will say one thing. Juan is a talker. He's more interested in talking about the cars he owns than business. He also wanted to have a coup on Alvarez. He is hungry for power. We did get wind that Alvarez is planning to use a cargo ship to transport the salvage. He has a few cargo ships that are run through a shell company that make the Miami to Colombia run monthly. We did a little research, and they never seem to go out full and have always lost money on the books. We think he's using them as a legitimate business to launder money."

"Makes sense. By the way, we already got the contents of the plane on board. It's cases and cases of lab gear and fifty-million dollars give or take." replied Rick.

"Give or take? I don't wanna know. I was planning to call you when you called. Juan picked up the first drop already on the little key you made the drop on. Can you retrieve the video from the island and forward it to us. If possible, just change out the flash cards. He may want to use the island again. Jules is an incredibly fast translator. She's wearing headphones now as Juan is talking to someone."

"She is amazing. Tell her I'll call her soon. Better yet, I'll just text her and she can call me when she's free. Alvarez gave us a week to salvage his plane wreck, but he still thinks we are waiting for an ROV. We are going to move the salvage we have already have to an unknown location in case they try and board the ship. Can you secure me a fast boat?"

"How fast and how big?"

"Something that can carry a large payload and as fast as possible."

"Hold on."

Rick waited on the line and Carson returned a minute later.

"The D.E.A. recovered a hydrofoil that once belonged to the Canadian government. It's the sister ship of the H.M.S. Bras d'Or. It's being auctioned off in Miami. I think I can pull a few strings and get you and extended trial."

"Do you know the starting price?"

"Hang on,"

"Starting bid is 1.4 million."

"This may be a silly question and I know the US government is not eBay, but do you think they will take a *Buy It Now* price of two million to take it off the market? We can pay cash."

"I'll find out and get back to you. Are you buying it or is Alvarez buying it?"

"That is in a need-to-know basis Carson."

"I read you loud and clear. By the way the boat is fifty-three meters long and has been clocked at seventy-two miles per hour."

"Damn, that's big and fast! Maybe we should just sea trial it. I have nowhere to store a boat like that. I'll talk to Gary."

"Whatever you think Rick. If they think you are serious, I'm sure I can arrange something. You'll have to pay for the fuel."

"No worries. Okay, let's chat soon."

Rick hung up and helped the guys store the last of the salvaged down below.

CHAPTER 10

J ules read the file she downloaded from A&A Bail
Bonds from Fort Walton Beach. The woman who did
not show up for her hearing was Kendra Jones. She
was twenty-five years old and had no prior arrests. The
man who filed the restraining order on her, however had
quite a long rap sheet including domestic violence and
aggravated assault. He had also been questioned about a
rape in another county, but charges were dropped. She found
it odd that a woman with no priors was charged in domestic
violence against a guy who had a history of violence. Something seemed fishy.

The address of the complainant was in a bad area of
Crestview Florida known for a lot of crime and drug abuse.
On a hunch she decided to case the house of the man with

Johnie and see if she could make any sense of it. She took Johnie's old work truck with him to area and staked it out. With a long lens she watched the house. They walked to the door as several cars pulled up, then they went inside and left shortly after.

Drug dealer.

She needed to pull a ruse and try and get close to the house. The only way was to follow one of the buyers and get their name as a reference. A dirty brown Celica pulled up and a young, strung-out looking Latina girl knocked on the door. Johnie wrote down the plate numbers as Jules used her camera and telephoto lens to get close ups of her face. They drove to the Okaloosa County Sheriff's department, and she called in a favor. One of the deputies had a crush on her and he ran the plates and gave her name. With a little flirting he told her that she had been arrested several times for the solicitation of prostitution. Her name was Rosa Casiata. Her street name was Kandy.

They drove back to the condo and Jules dressed the part. She used some dark mascara mixed with rouge to give herself dark circles under her eyes. She lathered on the makeup and lipstick and wore the sluttiest outfit she could put together. The mere sight of herself in the mirror made her blush. Once it was dark, they drove back to the man's house.

Johnie was nearby with a rifle just in case things went

sideways. Jules was packing her smallest handgun in a small purse and tucked the taser into her bra. She took a deep breath and knocked on the door.

"Whatchu want bitch?" asked the guy.

He was wearing a wife beater tank top under a plain long sleeve plaid shirt only buttoned at the top with slicked back hair and a black eye. He was full on cholo. He had a teardrop prison tattoo under left eye and his neck was completely tatted.

"Rosa sent me. I need a fix bad, man."

"Rosa?"

"Yeah Kandy, she said she was here earlier today?"

The man leaned out of the doorway and looked both ways, then let her inside.

"Whatchu need?"

"Let me see your arms!"

Jules held out her arms. There were no track lines.

"I just chase the dragon, I hate needles."

She tried look as serious as possible and desperate. The guy finally bit.

"How much you want?"

"I need a zombie hit. It's been two days,"

"We can make a trade," said the guy, as he looked up and down Jules body.

"Naw man, I have cash. I gotta works later anyway. I ain't in no mood to get down wif you."

"Ahaight"

"One fitty,"

He pulled out a large baggie with black gummy heroin in one hand and reached for the money with another. Jules unrolled the money and passed it to him.

"Aint chu Kendra's old man?"

He started laughing hysterically.

"I was but that bitch tried to steal from me, so I slammed my face in the wall and called the po-po on her and blamed her."

"I heard she was no show for court," said Jules.

"Yeah, she a no-show for life too. Now get out."

Jules scanned the room on her way out and saw a dirty smudged out .45 sitting on the coffee table. She had a sinking feeling she knew why Kendra didn't show up for her hearing. She was dead. She returned to Johnie's truck that was parked around the corner and drove straight back to Sheriffs Department. She found detective Roger Lindell in homicide.

There was a few hoots and hollers as Jules entered the station. She wished she had changed clothes but had a hunch.

"Detective, I think I know why Kendra Jones failed to appear in court," she said as she slid her case file to him.

"Why's that?"

"Because her boyfriend Carlos Aguilar murdered her."

"What makes you think that?"

Because of something he said. I have probable cause for

you to get a search warrant. She tossed the baggie of heroin on his desk. You'll find Carlos's DNA on this bag and mine. We just made a buy at his place. That's enough to search the place. If you test the .45 on his coffee table, I'll bet you a hundred dollars you'll find his prints, his DNA and high velocity blood spatter belonging to Kinda on that gun. He hasn't cleaned it for maybe, never!"

The detective typed on his laptop, leaned in closer then spun it around for Jules to see.

"He has several felonies on his record. We can get him just on a gun charge to begin with. Would you be willing to help us? I can get a warrant together and if you can make another buy, we can use S.W.A.T to take him down. Since you've been there once, he'll have his guard down."

"Perfect. Get the warrant, he's expecting me back in two days anyway."

RICK, Gary, and Possum drove to Miami in Rick's Bronco. Sebastian and Captain Larry P-Roy Lane stayed on the ship and protected the salvage. Carson had arranged for a sea trial for the go-fast boat. The plan was to load the salvage to the new boat off the ship and deliver it to a barge tied up in the mangroves in Everglades city. Gary bought the barge to use as a floating storage unit for anything he didn't want anyone to know about. It had ten stainless steel compartments and was damn near impenetrable with its heavy steel doors and cased in locks. The only way to get inside of it was with an acetylene torch. He kept it on shore near a stilt house he had purchased, and converted to a fish camp, for fishing excursions and had a guy who house sat and ran the trips for him. He routinely checked the barge for Gary. Until Gary told Rick about it, he didn't even know it existed.

Rick met with the man in charge of all auctions. It was a big salvage yard near Key Biscayne. They had military and civilian surplus cars, trucks, boats, office furniture. Damn near anything you could think of. They wish they had more time to hunt through the items but it wasn't that kind of day. The man's name was Charlie and he was a portly guy with a receding hairline. He took down all of Rick's info and told him it was a twenty-thousand-dollar damage deposit and he would be responsible for all the fuel. He also said that one of his employees would be on the ride along. It was company policy. After much negotiating and a thousand-dollar fuhgeddaboudit fee, he agreed to let Rick and the boys take it alone as long as it was returned full before closing time at 6:00pm. It was 9:15 when they fired up the massive hydrofoil. Gary called Sebastian and told him to start bringing the stash to the deck of Precious Jules. They had to load it fast. In an effort to save time, P-Roy weighed anchor and headed north, they could meet on the outside and save some miles. Precious Jules had already rounded Boca Chica by the time Rick got the hydrofoil into open water. At the rate the ship was moving he figured they'd meet somewhere outside of Marathon.

Rick pushed the throttle forward and the bow dropped then lifted and the foils came out of the water and the boat seemed to float through the waves. Before long they had hit sixty miles per hour and still had some headroom. He pushed the throttle a little more and they were doing sixty-eight and nowhere near the redline. Within an hour they were already past Key Largo and quickly approaching Islamorada. He called P-Roy and they had just passed Big Pine Key. Just as Rick thought, they'd meet near Marathon. Rick gave the captain the coordinates for Sombrero Key Light and told him to hold five miles East-Southeast of the marker. It was far enough offshore that they wouldn't be seen but not too far out of the way. He planned to take the hydrofoil under Seven Mile Bridge once loaded, and straight north, which was the fastest route up to Micmac lagoon where Gary's barge was located.

The hydrofoil pulled up alongside Precious Jules at 12:30pm. They were ahead of schedule. Sebastian drove the crane and they loaded all the cargo from Precious Jules onto the hydrofoil in under forty-five minutes. It would take much longer to load it onto the barge without the aid of a crane. They would have to do it by hand.

"P-Roy, can you get the ship back to Key West single handed?" asked Rick.

"As long as I stay on the outside, I should have no problem. I should be able her get into the anchorage alone and drop the hook."

"Sebastian, we need and extra set of hands, climb on."

Sebastian climbed down to the hydrofoil, and they once again were up to speed. Once they passed through Seven Mile Bridge he got it up to full throttle. Normally they'd have had to be careful as the water was skinnier on the inside but when the boat was at full speed it only drew a little over a foot on water. So, Rick kept the peddle to the metal and they made it to the Everglades in a little over an hour and a half. Sebastian rode the entire way on the bow pointing out crab trap buoys. They slowed down just before the entrance to Micmac lagoon, then idled slowly and side tied to the barge.

Sebastian and Possum stayed on the hydrofoil and Rick and Gary climbed onto the barge. They decided to use the number three middle barge compartment because it was closest to where they were offloading. Rick looked at his watch, it was 2:39pm. He knew they had to move the cargo and get underway by 4:00pm to be safe to get back to the auction yard by six. They had to hustle. They created a chain and passed each case and bag one by one down the line. Gary had climbed down into the compartment and Rick would drop the case down to him and he'd stack it. They did all the cases first as they were the most difficult and needed to be stacked. Once they got to the watertight bags Rick just tossed them inside the barge and Gary would just move them over and throw them into a pile. It was 3:50pm when the last bag was inside. Gary climbed up and locked it up tight. He stayed behind. He wanted to talk to his caretaker at the stilt house and booby trap the container on the barge. It wasn't something he wanted to be rushed doing. He'd use C-4 and a trip wire. If anyone tried to open container room number three, they'd be feeding the gators for some time to come in little bitty pieces.

Rick pulled away from the barge as they waved at Gary on the dock. They had to get to the fuel dock within an hour to be on time to the auction lot. Once outside of Micmac lagoon, Rick pushed the throttles all the way forward. The hydrofoil jumped out of the water like a rocket and within forty-five minutes, they were in sight of Crandon Park Dock Fuel Station. They topped off the tanks and motored along shore and arrived at the marina entrance at 5:40pm. They were tied up with fifteen minutes to closing time.

"Well, what do you think? You gonna be bidding?" asked the auction manager.

"I'm not interested, but thank," said Rick as he handed the keys to the man.

The disappointed man returned Rick's deposit after a short inspection and fuel gauge check of the hydrofoil. He never even noticed that Sebastian was there and now there were four of them instead of three. They all climbed back in Rick's Bronco for the long drive back to Key West. It had been quite a day.

Over the next couple of days, Rick and the boys resumed the search for the Mayan gold. It couldn't be too far from the sunken plane, so they started directly above it and towed the Proton 5 magnetometry fifteen feet behind the ROV. Possum had rigged it to feed any hits to the ROV instead of the ship and the ROV would send signals to the ship. One thing Possum was truly good at was redneck engineering. If Rick asked him to make something work that it wasn't designed to do, Possum would always find a way. After two hours of searching Rick let Gary take over operation of the ROV and called Jules. Gary had returned before sunup and slept in a little.

"Good morning sunshine. How's it going?"

"Good Rick. I'm so happy to hear from you. Remember that girl I was going after with domestic battery charge who didn't show up for her hearing?"

"Yeah."

"I think I know why. I think her boyfriend killed her."

"Really? Why?"

"He's a bad piece of shit. Covered in prison tats and has a record as long as my arm. I just have a gut feeling because of the way he laughed when I asked him about why she didn't show up for court. Now don't get mad but I am going to be working with S.W.A.T to take him down. My only role is to get him to the door. I'll be safe, I promise."

Rick took a deep out breath then let it out. He didn't want Jules to do dangerous things, but he also didn't want to tell her what to do and have her get bitter towards him. He centered himself and spoke.

"Okay Jules, just promise you will always have Johnie with you. Don't do anything without him. Okay?"

"I promise. We are doing the take-down tonight. I'll keep you posted."

Rick caught her up on the salvage and she told him that Alvarez planned to travel to Miami next week. He personally wanted eyes on the cargo. She got the feeling he didn't completely trust his underboss, Juan. She explained that he had it under control and had tried to talk Alvarez out of coming. After he hung up, he cursed in Spanish and Jules knew he was planning a scam on his boss. He was probably gonna try and say Rick shorted him and hide some of the cash bags. They all knew that once Rick made the final delivery that Alvarez planned to clean up any loose ends. They had to take him down and destroy the cartel or Rick, Jules and anyone else associated with the cargo would never be safe.

Johnie drove Jules in his old truck to Aguilar's neighborhood. They parked a block away and as they did they saw several undercover vans in the area. Drug neighborhoods were like the monkey's or birds in the jungle that warn other animals of an approaching tiger or other predator. Only the tigers now were the police. If they showed up in any black and white's Aguilar would never open the door and they wouldn't be able to get the jump on him.

Jules crouched behind the graffiti-covered wall of Aguilar's house, her heart pounding in her chest. The desolate Crestview neighborhood was cloaked in darkness, matching the chilling atmosphere that hung heavy in the air. She glanced over her shoulder at her trusted companion, Johnie, who stood vigilant, watching her back. They were about to execute a dangerous operation: taking down the suspected murderer Carlos Aguilar. Jules was no ordinary bounty hunter. She was highly trained and an expert in blending into the shadows and assuming different identities. Tonight, she posed as a street worker again; a drug addict desperate for her next fix. It was a role she had perfected; a mask that concealed her true purpose. As Jules leaned against the wall, she observed a car making a buy and told everyone to hold. Aguilar, a cold-blooded killer with a rap sheet a mile long, was inside the house. A dim streetlamp flickered, casting eerie shadows on the cracked pavement. Jules tightened her grip on the small pistol hidden beneath her tattered clothing. She knew the risks involved in this operation, but the thought of all the innocent lives that could be saved fueled her determination.

Once the buyer left, Johnie signaled Jules to move

forward. The plan was in motion. With each step she took, the weight of the task grew heavier. The line between reality and her undercover persona blurred, and she reminded herself of the mission at hand. She knocked on the door. A new stench of decay she hadn't noticed a few days before when she made her first buy, assaulted Jules' senses. Johnie maintained a discreet distance, ensuring no surprises awaited them. She decided not to enter this time and pressed her hand against the peeling paint beside the front door, listening intently for any signs of movement. The silence was deafening. Her heart raced as she prepared to confront the monster they had been hunting.

She knocked and suddenly a door creaked open. Aguilar emerged, a menacing figure with a face etched by years of brutality. Jules could see the darkness in his eyes, the absence of remorse. She knew that capturing him would be no easy feat. He tried to get her inside, but she knew from the smell, that a dead body was hidden somewhere in the house. She had no desire to join the late woman's fate.

Just as Aguilar was about to hand over the baggy, a synchronized crash echoed through the hallway. Johnie had snuck around back made his presence known, shifting the balance of power. Jules seized the moment; her training kicking in. She spun Aguilar around with lightning speed. The sound of approaching footfalls reverberated, growing louder with each passing second. The SWAT team pounced, surrounding Aguilar and ensuring there was no escape. The dramatic climax of their meticulously planned operation had been executed flawlessly.

As the handcuffs snapped shut around Aguilar's wrists, Jules felt a wave of relief wash over her. The nightmare was finally over. She glanced at Johnie and nodded. They had triumphed, together.

Jules covered her nose with a handkerchief and moved towards the odor. Inside of a closet in a trunk lay the body of Kendra Jones. She had a single gunshot from large caliber weapon to the back of her head. C.S.I. arrived quickly as Aguilar was carted off. They collected prints and DNA from the trunk and .45 still on the coffee table. The back bedroom appeared to have been cleaned, as the strong smell of bleach was detected. Aguilar was a pig and did a horrible job cleaning up the crime scene. He hadn't even cleaned his own weapon. Jules was certain a minute spec of blood spatter would be found on the gun. The back bedroom was a pigsty with clothes strewn everywhere and old bags of Taco Bell and Burger King sitting on the floor. She scanned the floor and baseboards then saw it. She called over one of the C.S.I guys and pointed at a small hole in the baseboard. After he took photos, he used a pair of needled nose pliers and knife to dig at the hole. He recovered a spent .45 slug. There was no doubt in Jules mind that Kendra's DNA would be on that bullet.

They followed the detective back to the Sheriff's Department and then headed to A&A Bail Bonds to get the reward.

Even though her bounty was dead, she earned the reward. She split it with Johnie, and they headed home. Jules showered and told Johnie goodnight as he slipped into the shower in their guest bedroom.

As Johnie was drying off his phone rang. It was a frantic Rick.

CHAPTER 11

Rick's phone rang about 9:00pm as he was munching on an apple in the galley of Precious Jules. He answered without thinking. It was Juan. There was no time to get Possum to record the call.

"How is the salvage going?" asked Juan.

"Uh, we haven't started yet. We're still waiting for the ROV replacement."

"I thought you were more resourceful than that. We want our property faster. I think I know a way to speed things up. I have something you may want in return."

"Rick, Rick, I'm sorry."

It was Jules. They had Jules.

What the fuck?

"If you touch a single hair on her head, I'll personally kill you with my bare hands."

"Calm down Mr. Water's. All we want is our stuff. You have three days now. We will trade your girl for the cargo, and you will never hear from us again."

He hung up before Rick could answer.

Rick immediately called Johnie.

"Johnie, they have Jules. How did they get her?"

"What?" I just spoke to her ten minutes ago. I was in the shower. Hang on."

Rick heard some rustling on the phone and few expletives and then Johnie returned.

"They cut a hole in the window of your bedroom. There's a perfect circle in the glass and it's unlocked. Jules said she was going to go to bed. I never heard a thing."

"How is that possible, there are a half dozen FBI agents next door and you were with her, and they still got her?"

"I know, I know. I take full responsibility."

"How the hell did they even know she was in Destin?" asked Rick.

"I have no idea."

"I need to think. I'll call you back."

Rick hung up and slammed his iPhone down on the table. He was furious and scared. He now wished he would've kept her with him instead of sending her up to Destin. He was beside himself as Gary and Possum walked into the galley.

We have a mole.

"What's up Rick? You look horrible," said Possum.

"They got Jules. I can't even wrap my brain around it."

"How the hell?..."

"They cut a hole in my bedroom window and unlocked it. Somehow, they managed to nab her without being seen or heard. I'm guessing they used a tranquilizer gun or stun gun. We should've never fucked with that plane. I have to get her back."

"We need a plan," said Possum.

Rick had Gary and Possum to follow him to the stern. They climbed on the dinghy and motored away from the ship.

"You two are the only ones I trust. We don't know that much about Captain Lane or Sebastian. I think one of them is a mole. Who all knew that Jules was going back to Destin other than us?" asked Rick.

"Could it be someone from the inside. The FBI?" asked Possum.

"Maybe. We know damn well it isn't Carson. I need to reach out to Carson and see if he trusts his entire team. Not a word of this to P-Roy or Sebastian. Let's act like its business as usual."

"Hey Sebastian. I think we should send the ROV over that area we just took the dinghy," said Rick as he motored back to the ship as to not arouse suspicion.

Rick disappeared down below as Sebastian and Gary moved the ROV into place for another scan. Rick paced back and forth in his cabin, his mind consumed by thoughts of betrayal and deception. The mysterious mole on the ship had to be discovered, and it was time for Rick to put an end to it once and for all. As he considered his options, again and again, two names stood out in his mind: P-Roy and Sebastian. Neither of them had been acting suspiciously lately, but they were still prime targets in Rick's mind.

Rick had come to trust P-Roy, but something had changed in him recently, a subtle shift in his behavior that raised Rick's suspicions. P-Roy had been spending more time alone in his quarters, avoiding eye contact, and seemed on edge about the current mission. It was as if he had something to hide.

Sebastian, on the other hand, had always been a wildcard. As the ship's do everything guy, he had access to various areas that would make it easier for him to carry out clandestine activities. As Rick delved deeper into his thoughts, he couldn't shake the feeling that the mole might be someone else besides the crew, someone from the FBI team that had been assigned to work with them. They were the only one's privy to their operations and knew the ins and outs of the crew. Rick couldn't help but wonder if one of them had been compromised, turning against them to protect their own interests. His mind was racing with possibilities when his phone buzzed, snapping him back to reality. It was Carson, the head of the FBI team assigned to their mission. Rick answered the call, his voice laced with urgency.

"Carson, we need to talk."

"I know Rick, Johnie just ran over and told me. My team was here and we didn't hear a thing. I'm so sorry they got Jules."

"I think we have a mole on the ship, and I have a strong feeling it might be someone from your team," Rick said, his words dripping with suspicion.

Carson let out a heavy sigh. "Rick, I understand your concerns, but I assure you that every member of my team has been thoroughly vetted. We are all working towards the same goal here."

Rick wasn't convinced. "Look, Carson, I respect your team, but we can't ignore the facts. The mole has inside information, and it's not a coincidence. Jules has been kidnapped, and someone told Alvarez right where she was. There's no way it was Johnie. He'd die to protect her."

There was a brief silence on the other end of the line, and Rick could almost sense Carson's frustration. "Rick, I understand your desperation, but jumping to conclusions without concrete evidence could be detrimental to our mission. We need to work together and find Jules before it's too late."

Rick took a deep breath, trying to steady his emotions. He knew Carson was right; they needed to approach this with caution. "You're right, Carson. We can't afford to let our suspicions blind us. But we need to step up our efforts to uncover the truth. Time is running out."

Carson's voice softened. "I know, Rick. We'll do everything we can to assist you. I'll personally investigate any potential leaks within our ranks. In the meantime, keep your eyes open and trust your instincts."

As Rick hung up the phone, he felt a renewed sense of determination. He couldn't sit idly by while Jules was in danger. He needed to find the mole, put the hurt on them, and rescue Jules before it was too late.

Over the next few hours, Rick intensified his investigation, discreetly observing both P-Roy and Sebastian. He meticulously documented their movements, searching for any evidence that would link them to the mole. He enlisted the help of his crew, ensuring that every corner of the vessel was monitored.

As the pieces of the puzzle slowly came together, Rick's suspicions began to solidify. P-Roy had been spotted sending texts, and Sebastian had been seen engaging in secretive conversations with unknown individuals. Rick wanted to confront them but knew better. If he did it may get back to Alvarez and he could end Jules.

In a tense showdown, Rick gathered P-Roy, Sebastian, and the rest of the crew in the ship's briefing room. The atmosphere was thick with anticipation and apprehension. Rick stood before them, his gaze piercing.

"I've called this meeting because we have news," Rick announced, his voice echoing through the room. Jules has been kidnapped in Destin."

He studied their reactions and they both seemed concerned and surprised. Not the reaction he was expecting.

He had a gut feeling now that neither one of them was involved. The tension was palpable as Rick continued; his voice filled with conviction.

"But let's not forget that the mole could be someone on the inside, someone we least suspect. The FBI team working with us has access to our operations, and it's a possibility we can't ignore."

The room fell into a heavy silence, each member of the crew contemplating the weight of Rick's words. In the midst of the chaos, Rick remained resolute. He would stop at nothing to uncover the truth, rescue Jules, and restore order to their mission. The hunt for the mole had reached its boiling point, and the fate of everyone on the ship hung in the balance.

"Rick, the day you sent Jules to Destin?" asked Sebastian.

"Yeah? Why?"

"A sudden recollection just came to me about the time I was at the Green Parrot. It was about my friend who informed me that Alvarez had knowledge of our discovery of his plane. This same friend revealed that one of the crew members, the unfortunate one who met his demise, had sent messages to several individuals about it. Furthermore, he cautioned that nobody aboard the vessel Precious Jules was secure. This revelation implied that Alvarez not only knew the reason behind naming the ship after Jules but also understood her significance to you. Perhaps there isn't a traitor among us after all; it's plausible that Alvarez simply connected the dots."

There was a long silence as Rick contemplated what Sebastian said.

"You may be right. Every crew member on the ship knew I just asked for Jules's hand in marriage at Mallory Square. I couldn't stop bragging about it. It doesn't take a rocket scientist to see how important she is to me. She is the perfect leverage. I guess it's time to make a deal."

Rick picked up the phone and called Juan.

"Juan listen up. I will deliver Jefe's property in three days. There is no way I can get it any faster. It's physically impossible. It's sitting at sixty-six hundred feet. I need proof of life. Every day at 8:00am, send me a photo of Jules holding up that day's U.S.A. today. Make sure it's clear so I can see the date. I expect a text as 8:00 am sharp."

Rick hung up before Juan could speak. It was a dangerous tactic, but he needed time to find out where they had taken Jules. Since they already had the goods, it would give them some lead time.

Just as Rick had hoped, his phone pinged at 8:00 am. He quickly opened it and there stood Jules with a sad look on her face holding a copy of the paper.

Rick rushed to the galley and met the boys over coffee. He forwarded the photo to all their phones.

"Why'd you pick the USA Today paper. Why not the Destin Log?" asked Gary.

"I'll tell you why", said Possum with a wink, as he spun his MacBook around and zoomed in. "Because the USA Today is sold on newsstands all over the world. The Destin Log isn't. Look closely."

Despite being aware, Rick couldn't resist and leaned in. Positioned prominently at the upper center of the newspaper, just above the USA Today logo, were two inconspicuous words: International Edition. It was most likely the Colombian version and they picked it up at a newsstand.

"Boys, we're going to Colombia. Where's your jet Gary?"

"It's in Destin. Clay is finishing up his helicopter training."

"Tell him to take a break and get to Key West. It's time to pay Alvarez a little visit. He won't be expecting us. Lock and load."

Rick and the guys filled up duffels will enough the ammo and firepower to take down the Sandinistas during the Iran-Contra affair. Sebastian took them to Nine-Tenths on the inflatable and they packed even more. With a little intel from Carson, they got the GPS coordinates of Diego Alvarez's home base in Colombia. He also found out that Diego's daughter was in college at the University of Bogata. She had a full-time security team guarding her. The one thing that

Rick knew about Alvarez is that family is important. He also knew that even if he gave him the recovered property from the sunken DC-3, he'd most likely kill Jules anyway. The only way he was ever gonna get Jules back, was a trade. Alvarez's daughter for Jules, even trade. The last thing Rick wanted to do was kidnap an innocent girl, but he had no other choice. He would never hurt her, but Alvarez didn't know that.

THEY LOADED the jet for Bogota. They lifted off just as the sun set. The flight would only take three hours and forty minutes. Once in Bogota they rented a Land Rover and checked into an Airbnb near the college. Carson had emailed several photos of Camila Alvarez. She bore a striking resemblance to Jules. Long straight hair with a thin muscular build.

The next morning after Rick got the text from Juan, Gary sat on a bench near the main entrance of the college hiding behind a newspaper. Possum fit right in and as a tenured retired professor managed to set up a class audit with the professor of anthropology. Upon meeting the professor and charming him, he had set up a guest lecture later that day. Camila would definitely attend, as it was her major, and it meant extra credit. They watched her leave her morning class and she was followed by three men who bore the look of secret service—Colombian style. Once she entered a new class they backed off and let their guard down a little. The best chance of getting her was during the lecture.

The lecture was scheduled to take place on the first floor of the tourism and development building, combining informative discourse with a casual social gathering adorned with snacks and punch. The attendance was expected to be minimal, with only a few students present. The plan was straightforward. Rick and Gary would hide in a closet within the women's restroom, to nab her once she finished her business. Meanwhile, during the meet and greet phase of the lecture, Possum would assume the role of punch server. Cleverly, he would infuse a small amount of Furosemide liquid, also known as Lasix, into one of the cups positioned closest to him. His intention was to ensure that Camila received this cup, and he knew precisely how to make that happen.

Rick and Gary positioned themselves ten minutes prior to the start of class, while a small group of students arrived shortly after. To Possum's surprise, two security personnel unexpectedly entered the room following Camila. Due to the class not being on the schedule, they had taken extra precautions. Sensing the potential threat, Possum swiftly alerted Rick via text about the uninvited company. Unfortunately, the closet lacked a lock leaving them vulnerable to inspection by the guards. In response, they quietly moved to the rear of the deep closet concealing themselves behind a shelf draped with cleaning supplies. Their safety relied on the guards not venturing fully into the closet. After a few minutes, Rick heard the door creak open and caught snippets of a conversation in Spanish as the guards. They forcefully checked each stall before eventually opening the closet door. Rick had previously unscrewed the bulb, rendering the closet dark. He overheard the frustrated sound of them attempting to flip the switch multiple times before they finally gave up and departed.

Phew.

Possum poured punch into each cup and passed out the glasses to the students making sure Camila got the Lasix cocktail. He introduced himself, as a translator relayed his every word.

"Welcome to my guest lecture, I appreciate you all attending. As I'm sure Professor Perez informed you, I teach at Rice University and today's lecture will be on the preservation of Archeological sites as related to development in the twenty-first century. Before I begin, a toast."

Ladies and gentlemen, let us raise our glasses in celebration of the fascinating journey through time that archaeology unveils before our eyes. Here's to the intrepid explorers who tirelessly unearth the remnants of ancient civilizations and breathe life into their forgotten stories.

To the archaeologists who meticulously sift through layers of history, decoding the secrets of the past with every delicate brushstroke and careful excavation, we salute your unwavering dedication and passion.

May your discoveries continue to bridge the gap between bygone eras and the present, enlightening us with profound insights into our shared human heritage. Let us cherish the artifacts that connect us to our ancestors and allow us to grasp the beauty of their existence.

So, let us toast to the archaeologists, the guardians of time, who unravel the mysteries of the past and inspire us to appreciate the rich tapestry of our collective past. Cheers to preserving history and preserving our sense of wonder!

He took a sip and saw that Camila and the rest of the class all did the same. Even the guards had a glass. As he began his lecture, he noticed Camila drink another sip of her punch. He knew it wouldn't be long until she needed to use the restroom. It was only a matter of time. About fifteen minutes into the lecture, he saw her squirming in her desk. She stood up followed by the guards. As she approached the ladies' room, she spouted out angrily at the guards, "¡¿Ni siquiera puedo orinar solo?!" which basically meant leave me alone while I pee!

The guards stood on each side of the door and waited. Rick and Possum quietly listened and when they heard the water running as she washed her hands, Rick slid out of the closet and behind her. He covered her mouth with a chloroform laden cloth. She collapsed in his arms. He quietly pulled her limp body towards the large window and Possum climbed out. Rick passed her limp body to him, and they tossed her the backseat of the Range Rover they had parked just outside the building. The building was off campus and at that time a day, had little to no activity around it. Rick texted Possum the signal.

"Will you excuse me for a minute. I'll be right back," he said to the class.

He slowly walked out of the classroom and as soon as he closed the door behind him, he sprinted for the exit. He dove in the back seat where Gary had propped up the unconscious Camila and they were out of sight and off the property in less than a minute. The only thing Rick regretted was not being able to see the looks on the guards faces when they entered the empty restroom with the closet ajar. Possum gagged Camila and bound her hands with heavy duty zip ties. On the way to the Airbnb, Rick stopped a picked up a copy of the USA Today. Once they were in the Airbnb and she was secured comfortably in a bedroom, Rick sat her down and explained to her that she would not be hurt. She was fiery and defiant but after struggling for a while, she finally gave up and relaxed. Possum held the newspaper in front of her as Rick snapped a photo with his phone. He texted it to Juan with just one word: Trade?

CHAPTER 12

Less than a minute went by, and Rick's phone rang.

"We aren't using burner phones anymore?" asked Rick with a laugh.

"You are fucking dead!" said Juan.

"Now, now, Juan, are you sure you want to talk to me like that? I do, after all, hold your boss's daughter's life in my hands."

There was a long pause on the phone.

"What do you want?"

"You know what I want Juan. I want Jules for the girl. Even trade. If you double cross me or hurt Jules, Alvarez will never see his daughter again. Well, that's not exactly true. I will send her to him in separate little boxes, one piece at a time. Do I make myself clear?!" exclaimed Rick.

He had no intention of hurting the innocent girl, but he

also knew Alvarez respected only one thing and that was violence. His reputation for violence was feared, even by other cartels. Rick also knew that he would never stop trying to kill Rick once he got his daughter back. The only way to stop him was to kill him or take him and his entire cartel into custody. He didn't care which, as long as he got Jules back.

"I want to speak to Alvarez. The next call better be from him. I'm tired of dealing with his underboss. You got that Juan. Have him contact me directly from now on. Comprende?"

Rick hung up. All he could do was wait. He knew Alvarez was not only a drug kingpin, but he was also a psychopath. He was afraid of what his next move would be. They had to lay low, there was no measuring how many spies he had in Bogota. They stuck out like sore thumbs. At least the Airbnb was a self-check-in and so far, they hadn't even seen a maid. He had made the reservation under an alias so they couldn't be tracked.

"How are we gonna do this trade? He's never gonna let us out of Colombia if we bring him his daughter," said Possum.

"You're right amigo. We're not gonna bring her to him. He's gonna bring Jules to us. Clay, is the jet refueled?"

"Yeah, it's ready to go. Where are we heading?"

Rick thought for a minute then said,

"Marcos Island Executive,"

"Okay, may I ask why?"

"Let me answer that one, Rick. I can read your mind. You

want to use Gary's fish camp as a trading point because that's where the cargo is. Am I right?" asked Possum.

"You are correctomundo my mind reading friend. If we can get the Feds to secure the area tactically, we can bust Alvarez on US soil and get Jules back without incident."

"But how do you know we can actually get Alvarez to show?"

"That's easy, we'll take a photo of his daughter sitting on the barge holding a USA Today. He *will* show. Once he lets Jules go at the airport, I'll give him the GPS coordinates of the barge. He'll get his daughter and get his property and then the Feds can nab him."

They tranquilized Camila and headed to the airport. Once airborne and out of Colombian airspace, Rick called Carson and told him he'd have more details for him soon and needed his help. Gary called his custodian at the fish camp and explained everything to him. The plan was far from full proof and Rick worried something could go wrong. He didn't trust Alvarez and still wasn't sure if there was a mole in the FBI. Rick called P-Roy to check on the ship and see if they had any visitors he didn't know about.

"Hey Rick, all good here. Pretty quiet. I gave Sebastian a few days off. There's no reason for him to just sit here and twiddle his thumbs. He went back to Key West until you need him," said the captain.

"Alright P-Roy, just sit tight. We should be able to resume the recovery mission in a day or two if all goes as planned."

Rick hung up and waited for Alvarez to call. They were almost near Cuba when his phone rang.

"Rick Waters."

"Mr. Waters, this is Diego Alvarez. I understand you have my daughter. That was not very wise Mr. Waters. Do you know who I am?"

"I know all about you. But you don't know much about me and trust me when I say it's in your best interest to accept my offer. Even trade. Jules for your daughter and you can have the entire contents of your plane. I don't even want a finder's fee."

He heard a little chuckle on the other end.

"What makes you think you can even get out of Colombia alive Mr. Waters. I have people everywhere."

"I figured that. Hang on."

Rick snapped a photo of Camila sitting in her seat with her feet and hands tied and made sure the window of the jet was in clear view. He texted it to Alvarez and waited. He could hear cursing in Spanish.

"Alright, alright. I accept your offer. When and where?"

"I'll assume you have a jet. Leave Bogota with a flight plan for Miami. Once you are airborne, call me back and I will tell you where to divert and drop off Jules. When she is safe, I will text you the GPS coordinates of where your property and daughter are located. You have my word."

"You give me no choice Mr. Waters. We will depart

within the hour. Once this is over, you better have eyes in the back of your head."

"Threat acknowledged."

Rick hung up.

"Change of plans. Fuck the FBI. I have another idea. I trust Carson but there's someone else on that team that isn't on our side. I feel it in my gut. We need another team. We need a different team for this sting. I'll call Carson now."

"Hey Carson. Are you alone?"

"Give me ten minutes."

Rick waited and his phone rang.

"What's up Rick?"

"Listen, I still don't know if one of my guys or one of you guys is informing Alvarez. You're the only one I can trust. How quickly can you put a team together and be in the Everglades? I have a contact for you there. I am trying to lure Alvarez there and he needs to go down. It'll take a day. I have some guys I worked with in Miami. I can rendezvous with them there and then head across HWY 41 and set up."

"We need special ops. I'm talking NAVY Seal type guys," said Rick.

"I gotcha. I can get some for-hire guys but they ain't cheap. A contact of mine in Ft Lauderdale runs a private security company. He can get anyone for a price."

"Okay they need to be heavily armed and amphibious. That area is snake and gator country. Once I give Alvarez the coordinates, there's no telling how he will approach the site.

He could chopper in or come by boat. I have no clue. They must be ready for any possible scenario."

"I'm on it. Give me a few hours and I'll get you the guys you need. Where are you now?"

Rick looked out of the window.

"We just past Guantanamo Bay to my left. Let's hope we can put Alvarez there soon!"

"Deal."

THEY LANDED at Marcos Executive Airport and secured two rental cars. Gary took off for the fish camp and Rick stayed behind. He texted Alvarez where to bring Jules. He was about two hours behind them, so Rick had Clay and Possum move the plane to Fort Myers with Camila still on board.

He was sure by now that Alvarez knew what he looked like; so he drove over to Hammock Bay Golf & Country Club bought a floppy hat and some sunglasses in the gift shop and a bright pink women's golf shirt and sun hat. The golf course was a flurry of activity as a tournament was happening. It gave him an idea. He rented a golf cart and drove it to the eastern edge of the golf course and parked it on Mainsail Drive at the western edge of the airport. He watched jets land and take off and kept his eye open for any plane with the tail numbers beginning with HK. One landed and he knew it was Alvarez. He texted Alvarez.

> *Walk Jules to the golf cart and release her. I have eyes on you. Once she is off the airport terminal, I will send you GPS coordinates.*

RICK WALKED to the edge of the golf course and hid in the shrubs. Within minutes Jules came down the street looking confused and scared. Once she got close to him, he moved out and signaled her to park. She ran to him and hugged him hard. He pulled her into the brush and handed her the shirt. She donned the hat and they stepped onto the rough and joined the crowd watching the tournament. He texted the coordinates to Alvarez. They blended in perfectly with the golf fans.

Alvarez texted back.

> *I'll be coming for you.*

Rick and Jules moved along the course with the crowd, following the golfer on the leaderboard. Once they got close to the seventeenth hole, they strolled towards the clubhouse and each picked up a golf bag left unattended. Rick looked all around and opened the back of the rented Escalade, loaded up the clubs as Jules got in the passenger seat. He had her lay the seat all the way down then pulled his hat down farther over his eyes and drove off. Once they got on I-75 he let her sit up.

"We're safe."

"No, we're not Rick. He will never give up," said Jules with tears of joy and fear mixing.

"Where are we going?"

"To a safe house. I'll put you there and finish this once and for all."

"Stop the car now! I'm not going to any safe house. I'm not leaving your side again. That's my final word."

Rick took the next exit and pulled over. He could see by the look in her eyes that there was no way in hell she was gonna let him leave her anywhere. Not even Fort Knox. He relented.

"Listen. I know you probably have a plan, but you have to listen to me. I overheard Alvarez. He always talked in Spanish, and I always responded in English as if I didn't understand. He doesn't know I speak Spanish. I did that purposely. He said his guy on the inside was gonna get the goods. He already knew where it is."

"Oh fuck. Gary's already there. I must warn him. He

grabbed his phone to call Gary and it rang in his hand. It was Possum."

"Rick, there's been an explosion. Gary is unconscious. His caretaker called me and said Gary saw someone climbing on the barge. He was running towards the barge and yelling for them to stop, then the barge blew up. The caretaker had just returned from a fishing trip. There is nothing left of the barge. Whoever was on top of that barge is gator food now. Was it Alvarez?"

"No chance, I literally just texted them the GPS coordinates. Whoever was on that barge was their inside guy. Probably someone from the FBI. Where's Gary now? He's on the way to Baptist Health Homestead by ambulance. According to caretaker the concussion blew him five feet backwards. He was unresponsive but breathing when he reached him."

"This is unbelievable. I don't know what to do. Keep me posted on Gary's condition," said Rick.

"Will do amigo. What are we doing with Camila?"

"Let me think. I'll call you back."

Rick slammed his hand against the steering wheel in frustration.

"I don't know what to do."

"You still have Camila. You still have leverage. Let's use it," said Jules.

"How?"

"He's gonna try and kill you, me and the rest of us no

ERIC CHANCE STONE

matter what now, but he still wants his daughter. Let's just use her as bait. She's all we have," said Jules.

Rick called Possum back.

"We're on our way. Make sure the jet is full and ready to go."

"Where are we heading?"

"Up."

Rick and Jules arrived at the PrivateSky Aviation Services in Fort Myers where the jet was parked. They climbed aboard and Clay filed a flight plan for Ft. Lauderdale. They would at least start heading that way. As the plane lifted off, Rick was deep in thought. They had to get somewhere where they could drop Camila safely and still capture Alvarez in the process. It was just then that he remembered to call Carson.

"Carson, call off your team for the Everglades. Things have changed. It's too much to explain now. Just keep them on hold for now. I might still need them."

"Okay, I'll have a team ready and waiting for you. They are in Lauderdale now. I'll have them stay put."

Ricks mind raced as he tried to come up with a way to get Alvarez. He knew once he had his daughter back, he'd be coming for them with everything he had.

"That's it! Fort Knox."

"What?" asked Jules.

"Oh earlier, when you were mad because I was gonna take you to a safe house, I realized you wouldn't let me leave you anywhere alone. Not even the most guarded place in the

U.S.; Fort Knox. Fort Knox is a euphemism for a place you can't break in or out of. It's an actual fort in Kentucky but if we can get Alvarez to something like that we can trap him. I know just the place. The vault at the Hard Rock Casino in Ft Lauderdale. Remember Jack Raynes, who owns that casino in Mississippi?"

"Yeah?"

"He's friends with all these casino owners. If I can get him to call the Seminole Chief Jim Billie to let us use the entrance to the vault. We can lure Alvarez inside to get his daughter and then shut the wall down and wait for the Feds to take him away."

"Won't she yell at him and tell him it's a trap?"

"You're right Jules. She will. I can gag her again I guess."

"I'm not an expert but I don't think the Seminole tribal leader is going to want a girl bound and gagged walking through his casino. What if I go inside instead of her? I'll sit facing the wall of the vault. He'll never know it's not her until it's too late."

"I don't like it," said Rick.

"We have no choice. He can't hurt me. He'll have to go in unarmed. That place has more cameras than, excuse the euphemism...,Fort Knox."

"Ahhh, you're getting it Jules. Right on the money."

"I'll call him now."

Rick called Jack Raynes and begged him for help. He

understood and said he'd call the chief. He called back a few minutes later.

"Hello?"

"Alright Rick, you are gonna owe me big time. I explained it all to him and he understands. He will meet you at the casino at his office later today."

"Thanks so much Jack. I do owe you big time."

RICK AND JULES took an Uber from the Fort Lauderdale Executive Airport to the Hollywood Hard Rock Casino and strolled into Jim Billie's office.

"Hello Mr. Billie. I am Rick Waters, this is Jules."

"Call me Jim."

"Okay Jim. Thank you for allowing us to make this happen."

"Since we did our hundred-million-dollar upgrade, we also had to upgrade the vault. It's more like a vault within a vault. The main vault is underground and has an exit that leads to where we have armored trucks. To get to the main underground vault, you must first pass through the vault hallway. Here let me show you."

Chief Billie clicked on a button and a screen came down. He used his laptop and started a video that demonstrated the design of the vault hall. The video was animated and subtitled.

As you approach the entrance to this subterranean vault the door itself, crafted from polished titanium alloy, stands tall and imposing—its surface adorned with an intricate pattern of laser-engraved symbols.

With the correct combination skillfully entered into the digital keypad embedded within the door, a resounding click reverberates through the hidden chamber. Slowly the door pivots on hidden hinges, granting entry into a dimly lit corridor veiled in an enigmatic ambiance.

The corridor leads to the heart of the vault hall, a circular chamber bathed in a soft, ambient light. The walls are armored with layers of reinforced steel, each panel gleaming with a mirrored finish. Embedded within this metallic fortification are an array of high-tech surveillance cameras, discreetly positioned to capture every movement with unwavering precision. In the center of the chamber, ensconced in an ethereal glow, stands the inner vault. It is a formidable structure composed of thick, impenetrable titanium plating, its size almost overwhelming. The sheer weight of the door alone, adorned with a meticulously carved crest depicting the casino's emblem, hints at the formidable security mechanisms within.

It is the secondary security feature that truly sets this vault hall apart. Along the periphery of the chamber, concealed within the seamless walls, lies a hidden network of sensors and mechanisms. At the first sign of a breach a series of metallic plates, invisible to the naked eye, begin to shift and slide; sealing off the entire hall from the outside world.

The walls, lined with an impenetrable layer of reinforced titanium alloy silently move into place, forming an impenetrable barrier. Within seconds the once-connected corridor leading to the outside world is now a sealed chamber, isolated from the rest of the casino. The vault hall becomes a fortress, impossibly secure and impervious to any unauthorized entry. No one gets in or gets out. Period.

"What about Jules. She will be inside the main vault?"

"As I said the main vault leads to where the armored trucks park. There is a manual escape door here. It is impenetrable from either side and only opened from the inside. She can walk right out, and you can wait for her there."

"Wow, just wow!" said Rick.

CHAPTER 13

"I have an idea. Whoever caused the barge to blow by getting the jump on us is dead and the salvage is blown to pieces. What if Alvarez thinks we moved the salvage to a more secure location. Like say?...Fort Knox or aka the Seminole Hard Rock Vault. That along with his daughter's return will entice him even more. As ruthless as he is, he is also greedy. There's no way he can know that we didn't move the stash before it blew up. All that stuff out there is in a thousand pieces. I wish we had kept the cash separate though. I'll call him," said Rick.

Chief Billie had set them up with a room in the casino. Possum and Clay were still on the jet with Camila. Rick dialed Alvarez's number and waited.

"Nice try Alvarez. I knew you had someone on the inside." said Rick.

"Where's my daughter?"

"I have good news for you. I have your daughter and your salvage. You don't think I was stupid enough to send you to a barge in the Everglades to get your money, do you? I moved it before you sent your guy there. I put it in a safe place. A real safe place. An actual safe. Meet me at the Hollywood Hard Rock Casino at midnight. You and I will walk in together and you can have your daughter and the stash. I have arranged for you to use the casino's armored truck to go wherever you wish."

Possum forced Camila to change clothes on the jet before he came to the hotel. He gave Jules her clothes right down to the same-colored ponytail holder Camila was wearing. When she turned around, she looked exactly like Camila from behind.

The Chief took Jules to the main vault and placed a chair for her in the center of the vault. He faced it to the back wall. She looked at her phone. It was 11:45pm. Showtime. The chief left the vault hall and proceeded up to the camera room. Rick sat at the big Wheel of Fortune inside the casino where he planned to meet Diego Alvarez. It was the only one in the casino and easy to find. He kept eying his watch.

"Mr. Waters?"

Rick spun around in his chair.

"Alvarez?"

"Yes."

"Follow me." As they walked through the casino Rick

scanned every inch to see if any of Alvarez's men were skulking around in the shadows. No one stood out to him."

They walked without talking and were let into the back room that led to the vault hallway. They were both frisked by casino security which gave Alvarez even more confidence. They turned left down the long hall, far in the distance inside the center of the big vault, Alvarez saw Jules sitting on a chair with her back to him.

"Camila, I'm coming," shouted Alvarez.

"This is as far as I go. Take your daughter and the goods in the truck. We are even."

Alvarez gave Rick a skank eye and proceeded to walk towards Jules. When he got within ten feet of her as Rick walked backwards a loud click sound came from the wall and the massive vault door slammed shut. Alvarez turned to run towards the entrance where Rick was, and the wall closed in front of Rick trapping Alvarez in the solid steel hallway. He put his hand to his forehead as he knew he was caught. Carson and three men appeared behind Rick and quickly took Alvarez into custody. His plane and men were seized at the airport. It was over.

Jules used the escape door in the main vault and soon joined Rick and the others in the casino. Alvarez was charged with money laundering, racketeering, human smuggling, and many other charges. He would never see the light of day again. Camila was returned to Colombia and released on the tarmac in Bogota. Gary's plane was wheels up before any

Colombian customs or immigration could even get near the plane. Clay refueled in Panama and returned to Ft Lauderdale.

Rick and Jules spent a few days in the casino, courtesy of Chief Jim Billie, the Seminole tribe, and the US Government. There was a two-hundred-thousand-dollar reward for information leading to the capture of drug king-pin Diego Alvarez. Rick donated the money to the Seminole Kids House for trauma and neglect on behalf of himself and Chief Billie. It had been one hell of a few days and all Rick and Jules wanted to do was lie in bed. Which they did.

GARY WAS STILL in an induced coma and had been moved to Cleveland Clinic Weston. The crew visited him but there wasn't anything they could do but wait. DNA from the explosion in the Everglades was still being tested. Whoever it was, tried to steal the stash for Alvarez but didn't know Gary had booby trapped it. When they examined the exploded barge, only a few burnt bills were left. All the lab gear was destroyed. The barge looked like it had been peeled open by God. There was nothing left to do but return to Precious Jules and continue the search and recovery they had started in the first place.

Johnie flew in and joined them in Key West. They all took the dinghy out to the ship and met P-Roy who had been getting tight with Chief. His flapped his wings when Rick and Jules climbed onboard. He was just like a dog—always happy when they came home. They decided to continue operations in the morning and stay on the hook for the night at the anchorage. During dinner Rick caught P-Roy up on everything that happened. He just listened slack jawed at the story. Everyone was there except Gary. Rick called the hospital and there was still no change in his condition. He was getting the best care possible but keeping him in a drug induced coma was the best way to protect his brain from swelling. They stayed up late into the night talking. One by one, they retired to their quarters. Rick and P-Roy were the last two left, and each other's yawns were addictive. Soon Rick joined Jules in their cabin and it was lights out.

The sun began its ascent over the horizon, casting a golden hue upon the tranquil waters surrounding the anchorage near Key West. The early morning air was laced with a gentle breeze, carrying with it the scent of salt and adventure. It was here, in this picturesque setting, that the mighty vessel, Precious Jules, prepared to embark on a search and recovery operation, bound for the vast open waters.

As the anchor was hoisted, the crew of Precious Jules sprang into action. There would be no hired hands-on deck this time. It was Rick and the gang only. No outsiders. The ship stood tall, its towering structure serving as a testament to its unwavering strength and capabilities. Painted in a pristine white, now adorned with the name Precious Jules in elegant navy-blue lettering along its hull that P-Roy had painted for them when they were away. The ship exuded a sense of purpose and determination.

The ship's decks bustled with activity as the boys scurried about, diligently executing their roles. The clanking of chains, the hum of engines, and the occasional cry of seagulls blended harmoniously, creating a symphony of anticipation.

The captain, adorned in his usual fishing shirt, stood tall at the helm, his weathered hands gripping the polished wheel with authority. His experienced gaze surveyed the surroundings, a chart spread open before him, tracing the intended course with expert precision. With a commanding voice, he issued orders, each word resonating with confidence and authority.

As Precious Jules gracefully glided away from the anchorage, the ship's engines roared to life, propelling it forward with a steady rhythm. The water swirled and churned beneath the vessel, leaving a temporary trail of frothy white wake in its wake. The sun's rays danced upon the surface, casting mesmerizing reflections that seemed to guide the ship on its destined path.

The search and recovery operation lay before them, a daunting task that demanded unwavering resolve. The crew's hearts were filled with a mixture of determination, hope, and the weight of responsibility. They were prepared to confront the unknown, to navigate treacherous waters, and to find solace in their unwavering commitment to their mission.

As they ventured farther from the shore, the horizon stretched before them, offering a vast expanse of limitless possibilities. Jule's eyes were fixated on the ever-changing panorama, scanning the horizon with sharp focus, keen to detect any signs of other boats.

Onboard, the ship's equipment and technology hummed with purpose. State-of-the-art sonar systems, radar, and other advanced devices stood ready to aid in the search and recovery efforts. Every tool was meticulously maintained, their sleek metallic exteriors gleaming under the sun's rays.

As Precious Jules sailed into open waters, its bow sliced through the gentle waves with a purposeful determination. The ship forged ahead, its every movement guided by the collective spirit of the crew. They were a team bound by a common goal, fueled by the desire to bring closure, and ready to conquer whatever challenges awaited them on this voyage of hope and determination. But most importantly, find that damn gold they lost once already.

They were shorthanded without Gary and the hired crew, so everyone had to pull their weight including Jules. She was more than willing to get her hands dirty. Rick was excited to have her to involved and to work beside her. Together the two of them did sweeping patterns in the inflatable towing the right yellow magnetometer behind it. The only hits they got were from the damn DC-3 that lay empty below. They expanded their search and after several hours returned to the ship to look at more options.

"Are you sure you are in the right area?" asked P-Roy.

"Of course, we are. I set the damn GPS myself when we dropped the gold overboard as the Coast Guard approached," replied Possum.

"What about set and drift?"

"Set and drift?"

"It's a nautical term. The only damn question I missed on the Coast Guard test. Anyway, what it means if you are on a course you must take in the current and speed. Set refers to the direction in which a current or wind is pushing or moving a vessel. It is the horizontal component of the movement caused by external forces. Set is typically measured in degrees from the vessels intended course or heading. For example, if a ship is sailing on a course of 090 degrees and there is a current pushing it to the north, the set would be described as "set north. Drift, on the other hand, refers to the speed at which a vessel is being moved off its intended course due to the influence of currents, winds, or other factors. It is the actual distance and direction the vessel or aircraft deviates from its planned route over a period of time. Drift is usually expressed in terms of knots or nautical miles per hour. For example, if a ship is sailing at a speed of 10 knots on a course of 090 degrees, but the combined effect of wind and current is causing it to move 2 knots to the north, the drift would be described as "2 knots north. You catch my drift?"

"Eureka! Let me see a computer fast," said Possum.

He opened a website and looked at the current averages for the time of year that they dropped the gold overboard.

"We were doing about six knots when we heaved it over right Rick?"

"The seems to serve my memory correctly."

"Look at the current. It's moving about five knots to the west with the Gulf Stream. So, if we dropped it at this mark and it fell sixty-six hundred feet with a five-knot current pushing against it. We are way off!"

"How far off?" asked Rick.

"I'm not sure, but since we were only going six knots when we pushed it over, there would be almost no forward momentum. So, if we head due west and use a zig zag pattern starting from exactly this spot where we dropped it, we have to find it."

"Wouldn't the weight of the gold be too much for the current?" asked Rick.

"Yeah, if it was just the gold bars. But they were inside that canvas, and it has drag which would cause it not fall straight down but down at an angle to the west. Get it?"

"Yes, I get it! Let's go Jules."

Jules and Rick hopped back in the inflatable and began sweeping. Rick drove and Jules used the compass to keep Rick on a western track. He went back and forth not missing and areas less than a football field wide for the magnetometer.

Possum watched them move further and further from the ship till they were almost a speck on the horizon. Thirty minutes later they returned looking defeated. Jules passed up the laptop to Possum and they all moseyed to the main salon.

"It's like trying to find a damn needle in a haystack huh?" said Possum.

Rick opened the laptop with the sonar 3D imagery on it, as Jules bit her bottom lip trying not to scream. Rick called possum over and pointed at the screen.

"What's that? A needle?" asked Rick.

"You found it?! Woohoo!" exclaimed Possum.

"I can't be certain without taking the ROV down, but it appears to be the only precious metal in a small tight area. The ping came from a depth of a hundred and forty-three feet. Look at the bottom topography from the sonar," said Rick as he changed screens on the laptop.

Possum leaned in and whatever it was looked to be right on the edge of the drop off. If it was a foot further over, it would be sitting at sixty-six hundred feet instead of close to one fifty.

"Let's get the ROV ready. I Sure wish Gary was here for this," said Rick.

"We all do," replied Possum.

P-Roy raised the anchor and position the explorer ship

about a hundred yards in front of the metallic ping and set the anchor again. Possum and Johnie lowered the ROV into the water and Rick took the controller and began the slow ascent. Once they got within a few yards of the object, an image became visible. As Rick slowly moved the ROV closer and shined the powered LED lights on it, they all cheered. It was evidently apparent that it was the same heavy mesh bags they had put the gold in when they dropped it overboard to avoid a Coast Guard inspection. They all cheered, hugged each other, and patted each other on the back. The needle in the haystack was found.

Rick maneuvered the ROV closer and now they could clearly see that the bag was dangerously close to the edge of the drop. He was extremely nervous about even touching it. If it fell off the drop, the recovery would be much more dangerous and difficult. He pushed the ROV from the deep end to the edge of the mesh bag and slowly opened the claws. He may only have one shot at it. He pushed ROV closer and clamped down on the mesh bag. As he lifted the ROV up the bag ripped, exposing the gold bars as it fell. A cloud of sediment kicked up blocking their view from the camera. They all held their breath. As the currents moved the sediment away from the lens, the bag came into view again. It was sitting on the very edge of the drop. It looked as if it could fall at any instant. As amazing as the ROV was, it wasn't exactly easy to maneuver and pick up things. Attempting the task was comparable to performing in front of a mirror, where everything appeared reversed. It was too risky to try another attempt. They had to find another way. Rick slowly raised the ROV and the crew brought it onboard and secured it.

"Dammit. Why does it have to be so deep? If it was thirty feet closer to the surface, I'd just throw on a scuba tank, and go down there and put a cargo bag around the gold and float it up by hand. It's beyond the safe limits of recreational scuba diving and we don't have access to a commercial dive helmet and rig."

Ricked looked over at Possum who was on his Texas Instruments calculator and scribbling numbers down. He was scribbling and scratching out numbers as fast as his brain would let him then he stopped and spun the notebook around to Rick.

"It's possible, but you will have to use Nitrox and make some insane safety stops," said Possum.

Rick looked down at what Possum a had written.

A compression table is provided for a 140-foot dive lasting 10 minutes. Following this dive, significant ascent stops would be required. The ascent would involve the following stop times at different depths:

40 feet: 10 minutes

30 feet: 23 minutes

20 feet: 41 minutes

10 feet: 79 minutes

The total ascent time would be 155 minutes and 20

seconds. This ascent duration corresponds to the outcome of the 10-minute dive.

"Rick you'd only have ten minutes at the bottom to secure the cargo netting and fill the lift bag. Then you'd have to start your slow ascent. We could position a couple tanks and regulators along the anchor chain, so you'd have enough air, just to be safe. It's dangerous but doable."

Rick looked over at Jules and the look on her face was obvious. She was totally against the idea. He'd have to work on her to get her to go along.

"Have you heard from Sebastian? He can pick up some Nitrox tanks for us in Key West," said Rick.

"I have texted him a few times. He hasn't gotten back to me," replied Possum.

"I'll call him. Maybe he got cold feet or just scared because of everything that went down," said Rick.

Rick pulled out his iPhone and called Sebastian.

"Straight to voicemail. I'm gonna head over to his place and makes sure everything's alright. I pray Alvarez's guys didn't get to him."

"Yeah, he's been a ghost since P-Roy gave him a few days off. I hope he's okay," said Possum.

"Johnie, what kind of range does the inflatable have? I wish Sebastian was here so we could just take the chopper to Key West."

"Rick, I think if we out a couple of Jerry Jugs of fuel on the rib, we can easily get to Key West. It's gonna be a choppy wet ride though."

"Aright who wants to go with me to get Nitrox tanks and check on Sebastian?" asked Rick.

Jules ran downstairs and returned wearing her foul weather gear with Rick's under her arm. It was settled without a word being said. Rick put all their electronics in dry bags and set a course for Opal Key Resort & Marina. The ride was brutal. They were splashed with salt spray the entire way there. It was miserable. Once they arrived, Rick stowed the foul weather gear and then grabbed an Uber to Sebastian's condo. His little VW was gone and there was a pile of mail in his box. Rick knocked a few times then peeked through the window. There was no one home. He tried his number again and it went straight voicemail. He had Jules keep an eye out and he picked the lock, and they quickly went inside. Nothing was in disarray. There was no sign of struggle which made Rick feel better. His laptop was sitting on the coffee table. He opened it up but it was locked with a password. It appeared he had just left. Rick had no idea why. He was turning out to be quite an asset to the team. There was a little notebook beside the laptop. Rick opened it and flipped it to a blank page. He heled it to the light and looked along the side. Ever so faintly he could see the impression in the paper.

ITA 223

He opened his iPhone and pulled up his FlightAware app.

He typed in ITA 223 and it showed no flights. He scrolled back a day, and it popped up; *ITA 223 Nonstop from Miami to Athens departed on-time at 9:23pm.*

"He's in Greece Jules. Something spooked him."

Rick looked in his bedroom and the closet was opened a few hangers were strewn on the floor.

"If I was to guess, he grabbed a few items from the closet and hauled ass to Greece."

"I think you're right Rick. Why isn't he answering his phone. I bet he removed the sim card and will get one in Greece. We just have to wait. He probably got wind that Alvarez's men were coming for him. Let's go get the tanks and head back. I don't know about you, but I think we should rent a bigger boat for the return to the ship."

"I'm with you a hundred percent," replied Jules.

They returned to the marina and secured a twenty-five-foot center console. Rick had six Nitrox tanks and regulators delivered from Capt. Hooks Diver Center and he and Jules secured them in the hold. The return trip would be faster and dryer. Rick locked up the inflatable to the dinghy dock and they slowly motored out to open water. Next stop, Precious Jules.

CHAPTER 14

J ohnie and Possum helped Rick secure the center console to the starboard side of the ship. They used extra fenders since it was a rental. Possum hoisted the tanks on board and rigged them up with the regulators. He fastened quick release nylon straps to the tank valves so Rick would secure them to the anchor rode on his ascent to bottom.

Rick would be using an Ocean Reef - GSM Mercury Underwater Wireless Communication Unit mask on the dive. That would allow him to communicate with Possum on the surface. It was a full faced mask with built in comms. They tested it on the deck of Precious Jules then again just below the surface.

"Rick, are you reading?"

"Loud and clear Possum. I'm ready to strap the reserve tanks to the anchor chain."

Rick ascended and Possum and Johnie slowly placed the tanks into the water. Rick used double the amount of lead he normally used so he could descend easier and faster. Descending at a higher rate of speed was much safer than ascending which could cause the bends or worse yet, air embolism. Rick began his descent with a thumbs up and blew a kiss to Jules. He secured a tank at ten feet, another at thirty then twenty and the last tank at forty feet. Then from the anchor rode, released all the air in his BC, and inverted and began kicking towards the bottom. The lift bag and heavy-duty cargo mesh was hanging from the left side of his waist and he had and extra deep water flood light dangling from the right side of his waist, and another in his left hand. He kept his eyes on his dive computer as he kicked towards the lost treasure.

The sounds of the bubbles had a different sound as he got to a hundred feet. The water sounded heavy and an eerie silence was all he could hear along with his bubbles. He passed a hundred and fifteen, then a hundred and thirty feet. He was now deeper than he had ever been on scuba in his entire life. That kind of depth was not intended for recreation divers. As he hit the hundred and forty-foot mark, the ripped mesh bag came into view. He clicked the timer on his dive computer that was preset for ten minutes. He had to work fast. He laid out the cargo mesh alongside the torn tipped mesh bag and began to place gold bars in the new bag. Once he got all the ones that were loose, he gently pulled the old bag closer to the new one and rolled it onto the flat part of the bag. Once he had secured each corner of the flattened bag into a cone, he wrapped a heavy-duty cable tie around it to keep the corners together. He was about to pull the rip cord on the lift bag which would instantly begin to inflate the bag and send it shooting to the surface. He reached for it and heard static over the headset. It was broken up.

"We have....", said Possum.

He was cut off and all he heard was static. He looked up towards the surface and saw a long boat's silhouette alongside the ship.

Rick finished Possum's sentence for him.

We have company.

Rick's alarm sounded. It was time to ascent. He dared not call out to Possum on the comm. He had no idea who had just approached the boat. Whoever it was they came out of nowhere and the boat appeared to be about thirty-five feet long and slender. Rick pulled the regulator from his mouth and added a little air manually to the lift bag. He slowly added air until the cargo became only lightly buoyant and lifted a few inches off the bottom. He pulled it along with him as he ascended much slower than his bubbles. Once he got to the seventy-foot mark. He kicked over to the anchor chain. He turned off his flood lights and secured the free one to his waist. He slowly ascended to forty-foot. He knew Possum would find a way to let him know what was going on up top. He secured the gold and lift bag to the anchor chain and it hung there. He had manually put just enough air into the bag to make it neutrally buoyant. He needed to decompress at that depth anyway so just hung on and kept an eye on his air gauge. He had about thirty percent of his air remaining but a fresh tank tied up next to him.

"Where is Waters?!" said a voice Rick recognized over the comm.

It was Juan.

"He's not here. He's on the mainland," said Possum.

That's my boy! thought Rick.

Possum must've wedged something into the handset of the transmitter on the surface and hid it out of site somewhere on the deck.

"Call him now! We are seizing this ship until he pays what was taken from us. I'm in charge now. I'm the new boss."

"Okay, okay, I'll call him," said Possum.

Rick listened as he held onto the anchor rode and decompressed.

"He's not answering. He must be on a plane. He had to fly to Tampa to pick up some gear. He'll be back tomorrow. His plane lands in a little over an hour," lied Possum stalling.

Before Rick had gone under, they had hooked the rental boat to the stern of Precious Jules. It was floating behind the ship about fifty feet back. Rick got an idea. He still needed time to decompress, so he unstrapped two of the full tanks and kicked up to thirty feet level, swapped his empty tank for a full one and tied off the other full one beside the one already in place. He tied off his dive knife alongside the two full tanks in case he had to stay there for a long period of time. His dive knife would be necessary if his instinct was right and knew how Juan would think. He returned to the sixty-foot level and slowly kicked in the direction of rental boat and stayed directly beneath the ship, out of site. Possum was talking a lot and must have looked over and spotted the air lift bag beneath the surface. He talked Juan and his men into the main salon.

Rick heard Juan say, "Tie them up."

Rick continued to slowly kick towards the rental boat. He was hanging on every word as Possum did everything in his power to stall Juan.

Once Rick had completed his decompression, he slowly ascended to hull of the ship and pulled himself along until he got to the cigarette boat, that was tied to the side of the ship. He pulled himself along the bottom of the hull of the cigarette boat, then opened his Leatherman and began to straighten the cotter pins on the dual props of the boat. Once straighten he pulled them out.

He left the props on the shaft then descended to forty feet and began to kick towards the rental boat with the neutrally buoyant float bag and gold in tow. With the stealth of a cat, he climbed onto the swim platform then rolled into the boat hidden behind the center console. He crawled along the sole of the boat, made sure the coast was clear then untied the painter and let it fall in the water. The boat began to drift away from the ship. He continued to listen to Juan and his boys threaten Possum and the crew through the comm he removed from the dive mask. Once he was about four hundred yards away from the ship, he pulled up the gold from down below utilizing the anchor winch. He stowed it onboard and fired up the engines and sped towards Key West.

Back on the ship Possum saw the boat floating away and did everything in his power to keep Juan from noticing. One of Juan's men realized the center console boat was gone and came in yelling to Juan in Spanish.

"Where is the little boat that was tied to the stern?" asked Juan angrily.

"Huh?" asked Possum trying to act surprised and oblivious.

"The boat, the little power boat is gone. Is Rick Waters on that boat. I will kill all of you!"

"No! Rick is on a plane. Dammit Johnie, what kind of knot did you tie when you hooked up the power boat to the ship?" asked Possum.

"Uh, uh, just a regular knot why?"

"The damn boat came untied. That was rental. I swear Juan Rick is on a plane, untie me and I'll show you on my phone. He's on a flight from Miami to Tampa. If you untie me, I'll call him again."

"I'll call him myself! What's the number."

Possum gave him Ricks cell number and knew his phone was in his cabin charging. He prayed it was on silent. Juan called the number, and it rang a few times and went to voicemail. Juan left a message.

"Call if you want your friends to be okay."

He slammed his phone down in frustration.

RICK HAD to get a message to Possum somehow. He remembered he still had the burner phone in his ditch bag that Juan had originally left for him. He sent a text to Possum hoping he'd see it.

> *Two Tanks/Knife*

Once he got to Key West, he motored up to some mangroves and hid the gold in the mud making note of the location. It was time for the cavalry. He called Juan.

"Juan it's Rick Waters."

"Mr. Waters, so nice of you to finally return my call. Now you listen I'm only gonna say this once. I am the new boss now that Alvarez is in custody. You can't stop us. As a matter of fact, I should thank you. I was planning on moving up the ranks and taking out Jefe myself. I deserve to be the boss now. That was stupid of you to blow up my property. You owe me sixty-million dollars. If you want your friends, get me the money, otherwise I will weight them down and push them overboard myself."

"Please don't hurt them. Especially Jules. I can't get that kind of money fast. I'll make you a proposal. If I bring you one million dollars, will you let me have Jules. You can hold on to the crew until I get the rest. It will take me a few days."

"When can you get the one million?" asked Juan.

"I can get it by tomorrow morning."

Rick knew he only had one chance at this, and prayed Possum saw his message. If he did, he would know what to do. He drove the rental boat straight for the Coast Guard station and didn't slow down. That would get their attention.

"You are in protected water, turn around immediately!" said a voice from a loudspeaker.

Rick turned off the key to the boat and raised his arms in the air. Within minutes he had been boarded with guns in his face.

"Don't move, you are under arrest by the US Coast Guard."

"My name is Rick Waters, and this is an emergency. Contact Chief Petty Officer Higgins, he knows who I am."

They place handcuffs on him and pulled the boat to the dock. Two men escorted him to the main Coast Guard building and put him in a cell. He just kept telling them to contact Higgins. Chief Petty Officer Higgins arrived about fifteen minutes later.

"Chief Higgins, I'm Rick Water, you were in charge of the inspection of my charter boat Nine-Tenths several months back. We were the ones who got towed in and had bow damage from Venezuelan pirates."

"Yes, I remember, what is this about?" he said with tone of frustration.

"I need your help. My fiancé and crew are being held on board my research ship, Precious Jules, several miles off of the coast of Key West by the Colombian cartel now being run by Juan Esteban. He has assumed leadership after the boss Diego Alvarez was taken into custody by he FBI. I have a contact in the FBI. His name is Carson Peters. Call him now. He will verify everything. I have a plan, but I need back up."

"Okay Mr. Waters, hold tight and I will check this out."

"Please hurry," implored Rick.

The doors of the cell opened, and Rick was escorted to Higgins office.

"Mr. Waters, I spoke with Mr. Peters, and he verified what you said about Alvarez being in custody. He was unaware that Juan Esteban had taken over the cartel."

"Yeah, we all were. That just happened. I have spoken with Juan, and he wants one million dollars to release my fiancée. Once she is in safe hands, I have a plan and timing will be crucial. These guys are heavily armed, and you will need a lot of firepower to take them down. I know how to get my friends safely off the ship. Once Jules is safe and they are off the ship I will signal you. My crew will need an amphibious rescue."

"We have a fully armored cutter in port and two H-65 rescue helicopters. That won't be an issue."

"I know for a fact that Juan and his crew have files of shipments on his cigarette boat, If you can seize that boat you will have everything you need to take down the cartel. Juan is power hungry but not the brightest bulb. I have audio recordings of them talking to the former boss about shipments and plans to go into the Fentanyl business. We even have some proof of a lab they plan to build. It is a strong case."

"We will work with your contact in the FBI and bring in the ATF and DEA if what you say is true. Once you seize that cigarette boat and review our photos and videos of the cash and laboratory supplies, we recovered from one of their trafficking planes, you will have an airtight case. It unfortunately was mostly destroyed in an explosion, but I know you can still find remnants at the site, and I will give you the location. You must trust me. My fiancée and crews lives are hanging in my word."

"Alright Mr. Waters. Let's get this operation underway. What do you need first? I need one million dollars in untraceable bills. I have already set up that trade to get my fiancée off the ship. It's step one. It's a good will gesture and I will gain Juan's confidence if we can make that happen."

"One million dollars? Is that all?" asked Higgins sarcastically.

"It's a start. He wants sixty-million but if this goes as planned, he'll get nothing and you can take him down before their Fentanyl operation even gets off of the ground in Colombia."

Rick gave Higgins his burner phone number. Higgins got on his phone and called DEA. The Coast Guard and DEA often worked side by side because of tall the drug trafficking on the Florida Straits. Rick needed guns and knew exactly where to get them. He called Clay.

"Clay it's Rick. Bring the jet to Key West. Before you leave, go on board Nine-Tenths and get the three black duffle bags under the main salon couch. Do it now, I'll explain when you get here. I'll meet you at the airport. How long will it take?"

There was short silence as Clay was thinking.

"I can be there in three hours if I leave now."

"Make it two and a half."

Rick hung up. The jet was sitting on the tarmac in Destin and Nine-Tenths was only a couple miles away in the slip in Destin Harbor. He had faith Clay would hustle. Rick took an

Uber to the Airbnb in Key West and fired up his Bronco. He drove over to Capt. Hooks dive center and rented a full Nitrox rig and three Spare Air units. He got a text from Clay that he was on approach. He looked at his watch. It had only been two hours since he called Clay.

Atta boy!

Rick sped to airport and met Clay. They loaded the duffels full of guns in the Bronco and took off for the Coast Guard Station. Once they arrived it was a hurry up and wait situation. Rick had to sign more paperwork than he would for a home refinance to take possession of a million dollars from the DEA. Once all the paperwork was complete and he was vetted, they boarded the rental boat and motored out of the Coast Guard Station bound for the ship offshore. He called Juan.

"Juan, I managed to get the first installment faster than I anticipated. Even trade—Jules for the million. Look, you are a businessman and so am I. We can do this in increments. One million for Jules, then ten million for each of my crew and the final payment of forty million for the captain. No funny business and you can be on your way in a few days. Deal?"

"Why not all of it now?" asked Juan.

"Juan, I have to have the money wired from my offshore account in the Cayman Islands. Then I must sign for it and go to the bank. It takes time. This first million came directly from my retirement account at SunTrust. I don't keep that kind of money in US Banks."

"Okay but if you try anything, I will send your crew to the fishes. It's impossible to swim with ankle weights and their hands tied. It will be a terrifying death. Do I make myself clear?"

"Loud and clear Juan."

"Call me Jefe from now on."

Jesus

"Okay Jefe, see you in about two hours."

Rick motored out towards the ship. He had Clay hide under the center console when they got close as Rick dialed Juans number.

"Jefe, I am approaching from the south. Do you see me?" asked Rick.

Rick had binoculars looking towards the ship and he could see Juan looking his way with binoculars as well.

"Yes, come along side slowly."

Rick tucked a .45 in the back of his waist and when he got close to the ship and idled up slowly. He held up the case of money.

"Throw it on board."

"Jules first!"

Juan's men all had automatic assault rifles aimed at Rick as Jefe pushed Jules towards the port side gunwale. He cut the zip tie on her hands and she climbed onto Rick's boat as he tossed the case onto the deck of the ship. She wrapped her arms around him and nearly squeezed the breath out of him.

"I've already started the wire transfer. SunTrust said it will take a few days to have that much cash delivered from the wire. I should be able to bring first ten million to you tomorrow night. The rest will take a day to two for each transfer. Believe it or not banks in Key West don't have sixty-million sitting in their vaults. It must be delivered by armored truck from Miami."

"Bring the first ten million by tomorrow night or I will push one crew member off at a time."

"I will bring it. Just be patient."

Rick and Jules motored out of sight.

"Did Possum see my message?"

"Yes, when he was asking Juan if he could call you, he picked up his phone. His hands were bound like mine in the front, but he was able to grab the phone. He saw the text before Juan snatched the phone away. He whispered in my ear. Scuba Tanks. What did that mean?"

"I'll explain later. We are getting you to safety. Do not argue with me. You are staying at the Coast Guard Station until Juan is in custody or dead. Please just go along, okay Jules?"

"Okay Rick," she said.

It was obvious she didn't want to be separated again but she trusted Rick. She also knew she would be out of reach of any of the cartel at the Coast Guard Station. Just then, Clay popped up from under the center console.

"Surprise!"

"Clay? What are you doing here?" asked Jules.

"Assisting your crazy husband to be I guess."

Rick had no intention of bringing any more money to Juan. He did, however, plan to save the crew and knew exactly how. Once they arrived at the Coast Guard Station.

CHAPTER 15

The sun had set in Key West as Rick kissed Jules goodbye. They put two guards on her room on the second floor of Coast Guard building six. It was time to set the plan in motion. Rick and Clay proceeded to Chief Higgins' office and met the team leaders of the ATF and DEA. This joint operation meant a lot to the US Government. All Rick cared about was getting his crew out of harm's way. Rick gave Higgins a flash drive with all the conversations and video they had gotten from Juan's cigarette boat and the original drop of some of the lab equipment on East Bahia Honda Key.

The video of Rick and Sebastian placing the lab gear and then Juan retrieving it later was enough to seal the deal. Both DEA and ATF were in with any resources needed. Rick laid out the plan. Everything involved timing. He wanted the cutter to ready to roll to seize the cigarette boat. He needed airpower to send Juan and his boys scurrying. The plan was simple now that Jules was safe. He was gonna tell Juan to go get fucked. He knew what he would do and would be prepared. They waited until the sun was completely gone and the stars held court over the sky.

He dressed in a bright red shirt and beige jeans and gave the same matching clothes to Clay. Clay wore a heavy bullet proof jacket beneath his red shirt. With the DEA and ATF in place hovering in twin H-65 Coast Guard helicopters a few miles from the ship. Amphibious Coast Guard rescue swimmers were in a third chopper. The cutter was far enough out that it couldn't be seen by anyone on Ricks ship. Rick motored towards Precious Jules. When he got within a few hundred yards he called Juan.

"Juan, we have a problem. I couldn't get the ten million tonight. It will have to be tomorrow. Please just give me Johnie or Possum in good faith. I promise you'll get your money."

Rick idled sideways about thirty yards from the ship.

"I guess you think I'm some sort of fool. I'll give you Johnie. But you're gonna have to fish him off the bottom!"

"Wait, wait, I'll get the money."

"This will ensure that you get the money. Johnie's done."

The deck lights of the big ship came on and two men walked Johnie, Possum and Capt P-Roy to the gunwale. Rick could see they were putting weights on their ankles and his hands were bound in front of him. He struggled as they cut the zip ties and moved his arms behind his back and rebound him.

"Shall I flip a coin and see who's first? Let's see if any of your friends can swim."

"Fuck you Juan, the deal is off. I'm coming for you!"

Rick started firing his pistol in the general direction of the boat as he moved to the stern and climbed on the swim platform, then laid down.

He had preset a text message for the Coast Guard in charge of the operation. He pushed send.

Now!

Clay stood up from under the center console and started firing his pistol in their direction hitting the water to make sure he didn't accidentally hit any of the crew on the ship. He pushed the throttles forward and shot towards the ship as he fired.

"Now Rick!"

Rick rolled off the back of the dive platform and underwater as Clay got within ten feet of the ship firing his pistol. Bullets shattered the fiberglass on the hull of the boat as he tuned the wheel hard to port and just missed striking the ship. Clay slammed the throttles forward to get as far from the onslaught of bullets as possible. Both outboards had taken fire and smoke was billowing from them. Soon the center console boat slowed to halt as the motors gave out. Oil leaked into the water and Clay was adrift.

Juan's men pushed Johnie, Possum and P-Roy off the ship into the dark deep water. They began to sink quickly holding their breath. Rick kicked with everything he had and got to P-Roy first. He handed him a Spare Air and cut the zip tie from his hands and released the ankle weights. The deck lights of the ship allowed him to barely make out their shapes. Rick motioned for P-Roy to swim towards the anchor chain. He began to kick towards the tanks Rick had secured to the chain. Rick was sure now that Possum had told them of the plan.

Rick scanned the water below for Possum, he was going down fast. Rick dumped all the air out of his BC and kicked with his fins as hard as he could. He put the Spare Air in Possum's mouth and dropped his weights. Johnie was the first to go in and was already down about sixty feet. There was no time to cut Possum's hands free. With every ounce of energy he had, he kicked down towards the sinking Johnie. When he got to him, his eyes and mouth were wide open. He had drowned. Rick grabbed him and kicked towards Possum and pointed upward. Possum managed to kick towards the anchor chain and P-Roy used the knife

Rick had hung there earlier to cut his hands loose. They both switched to the two scuba tanks hanging from the chain.

Bullets sprayed the surface and looked like little missiles flying through the water from the glow of the deck lights. Rick kicked towards the surface with Johnie's limp body in tow. As she broke the surface, he saw helicopters approaching.

"This is the DEA, surrender at once," rang out from one of the choppers.

Rick took off his BC and fully inflated it as he put it on Johnie. He began CPR, blowing into his mouth. He was unresponsive. There was no way to give him heart compressions on the water. Juan and his gang climbed onboard the cigarette boat and Rick heard the engines roar. The boat revved up but wasn't moving as the propped slid off the shafts and began to sink. Juan's men fired at the choppers, and they returned fire. A wall of bullets from a .50 cal shattered the boat and one of the men fell off the boat and began to sink as blood shot out from his chest. Juan raised his arms and placed them behind his head.

Two swimmers hit the water just a foot from Rick and they placed Johnie in a basket and hoisted him to the helicopter. Rick dove down to Possum and P-Roy and helped them to the surface. The swimmers assisted them to the chopper, and they revved up and headed for Key West. As they were leaving Rick could see the Coast Guard cutter approaching his ship. He knew Juan and whoever was still alive would be in custody shortly.

One of the Coasties was doing CPR on Johnie. He was not responding. They ripped open his shirt and place the paddles on his chest. Tears were dropping down Ricks face as they worked on him. He was praying like he never had before.

"Clear!"

They blasted his chest with the paddles and his entire body lifted up and then back down an inch up of the floor of the chopper.

"Again!"

He rubbed the paddles together then pushed the buttons and gave him a massive jolt. His head jerked forward and then he turned his face sideways as saltwater spewed from his mouth and he coughed. He was gagging and coughing as he gasped for air. His eyes partially opened, and he looked disoriented.

The Coast Guard medic on the chopper took his vitals managed to stabilize him. Once they arrived at the station, they put him on a gurney and rolled him to a waiting ambulance. Johnie was going to live. They also took, P-Roy and Possum in for observation. Clay had been given a lift with the Coast Guard once they found him on the rental boat adrift. He was in perfect health and resting in room 606 in building four. Rick and Jules weren't allowed to travel as the DEA, FBI and Coast Guard wanted to debrief them. Since Higgins was on point, he started.

"Great effort there, Rick. I'm still unclear what went down but the scuttlebutt is that you pulled off one hell of an amphibious rescue."

"I couldn't have done it without the support of team, Chief Higgins, the DEA, and FBI. Your Coast Guard swimmers are fearless!"

"We train all the time for water rescues. They were just doing their job. So, to update you, we have Juan Esteban in custody. He has a gunshot wound to his right shoulder and his foot, but he will be fine. Two of his accomplices are dead, and the third guy just arrived at Lower Keys Medical Center in critical condition and may or may not pull through. We seized the cigarette boat. We will have to tow it as both props are missing. I don't suppose you have any ideas how that happened?"

"Poor maintenance?" asked Rick with a grin.

"Hi Mr. Waters, Mrs. Waters I am agent Donahue with the FBI. I oversee the task force."

"Not yet, interrupted Jules. I'm still Jules Castro. We are engaged," said Jules as she waived her ring proudly.

"My mistake. Anyway, as I was about to say, we are going to push hard on Juan Esteban to flip and testify against Diego Alvarez. The Colombian government is watering at the mouth to try Alvarez as a serial killer. Not in the true sense but they believe he's responsible for over fifty, maybe more deaths in Colombia alone. We gathered a ton of evidence about the cartel's intentions to begin a Fentanyl operation.

And all the data on Esteban's laptop about their shipping company which we know was a money laundering business is enough to put Alvarez away for life. With Esteban's help, it's likely Alvarez will never see the light of day."

"What about Esteban, are you giving him a sweetheart deal?" asked Rick.

"If it goes the way we plan, he will get a better deal but he will do hard time. If we can take down the entire cartel with the help of the Colombian government, it's a solid win on the war on drugs. You did this country a great favor Mr. Waters."

"I can't take all the credit. It was my entire crew and your teams that made it happen."

"Regardless of that, I am going to ask the president to consider you for the Presidential Medal of Freedom."

Rick was speechless. He just couldn't make words come out of his mouth.

"Your entire crew will be honored as well. We will be in touch with you. I'm going to have to ask one more favor. We might need you to testify in Alvarez's trial. Are you willing to come to D.C. and testify?"

"Just say the word and I'll be there. I have a favor to ask myself. I need you to keep Jules's name out of everything. Her family still lives in Colombia. You know as well as I that someone will be coming up the ranks even if you destroy the cartel. Their reach is deep. Cousins will be coming out of the woodwork and the cartel will rebuild. That last thing I want is payback to anyone in Jules family. Can you promise me that?"

"I can make her testify. I could subpoena her, but I won't. If you are willing to testify we will be fine along with all the evidence we have collected. I'm almost positive Esteban is going to flip, and his testimony will seal the deal."

They continued to get info from Rick and Jules; and, after an hour, they got the update that Johnie was fine—as well as Possum and P-Roy. They would all stay overnight for observation and had two armed guards at his door in the hospital. The Coast Guard set up rooms for Rick and Jules for the night. Rick called the hospital in Miami to check on Gary. He was told there were signs of improvement and that he would likely be brought out of his coma in the next twenty-four to thirty-six hours. He planned to call back the next day with the hope to go visit with him soon. He hung up then remembered the gold. It kinda hit him like a freight train. The GPS on the rented boat that was now in Coast Guard possession and riddled with bullet holes held the lats and longs of the gold Rick had hidden in the mud of the mangroves. He couldn't do it tonight even if he wanted. He glanced at it watch and it was 3:15am. He needed sleep. They both did. The next morning Rick walked down to Chief Higgins' office.

"Knock, knock. Excuse me Chief Higgins. Are we under any kind of house arrest or anything?"

"Of course not, we just thought you'd feel safer here. If you'd be more comfortable somewhere else, I understand. I can have set up a security detail for you. Until we put this cartel to bed, you are our number one witness."

Rick thought about it for a while.

"Okay, we have an Airbnb rented. It's just sitting empty on the other side of the island. If you can put a couple of you armed guys there, we will be fine. Can you arrange transportation for us? I can't even remember where the hell I parked my Bronco."

"It's sitting right out front Rick. I can have my boys follow you."

Rick shook his head like he was trying to shake off all the confusion.

"Okay, we'll get our stuff together. Can you just arrange transportation for Clay, Possum and P-Roy to the Airbnb as well?"

"No problem. You can all rendezvous there," said Chief Higgins.

Rick got permission to reboard the rental boat. Some of his personal items were still on board. When he was not being watched, he took a quick photo of the GPS coordinates for the gold he had hidden. It was time to salvage it one last time! Once back at the Airbnb, Rick and Jules showered and got into fresh clothes. It was midafternoon when Possum and P-Roy arrived.

"Well look what the cat drug in," said Rick.

"Ha-ha. At least you didn't have to eat rotten hospital food. It sucked. I'm starving," replied Possum.

Rick ordered pizzas for everyone, including the guards out front.

They all talked about the mission and Possum made Rick swear he'd never have them be thrown off a boat wearing ankle weights ever again. He couldn't swear to it but said he'd do his best to make sure it never happened again. After the late lunch Rick motioned for Possum to follow him. They proceeded to the back bedroom here Rick could talk without the guards out front hearing.

"Listen, I'm gonna sneak out tonight after dark. They will probably do a guard change around 10:00pm, so I'll go after that. In case something happens to me, here is where the stash is," whispered Rick as he handed Possum a small piece of paper with the GPS coordinates to the gold he hid.

"I need the keys to the Gary's Bronco. The guards know mine. Where is it parked?" whispered Rick.

"It's on the north end of the street on the corner of South and Whitehead. I'll get the keys. Do you want me to go?" asked Possum.

"No just stay here and keep an eye on Jules. We aren't under house arrest but the less these guards know the better. If I can go out of my bedroom window and get down the street and back, it'll be a much better plan."

"Where are you going to put it?" asked Possum.

"For now, I'll keep it with us, so I'll text you just before I get back and you can help me pull it into bedroom from the window. Once the heat is off, we can put it in a safety deposit box in Destin. It'll be safe there until we can find a buyer."

"I like that plan."

"I will be muddy as hell when I get back so have some towels ready to place over the window seal and I can do a load of laundry once we secure the gold. If all goes as planned, I can be back in bed by midnight."

They all enjoyed a day off and lounged by the pool. The back of the Airbnb was surrounded by a six-foot cement wall covered in ivy. Chief Higgins had arranged for two armed guards. When the gang went to the pool. One stayed out front, and one guarded the rear of the property. After dinner they all watched a movie in the great room and shared some food with the guards. Just as Rick thought they had a guard change at 10:00pm. So, once they were in place, Rick went into action. He wore all black and a dark hat. It was an overcast night, and the streetlights were barely bright enough to cast shadows. Once he slid out of the beck bedroom window, he scaled the ivy-covered wall behind the pool and jogged down to Gary's Bronco.

Following the GPS on his phone, he backed up the bronco into the mangroves. It was only about fifty yards from where he parked to where he had buried the gold but it would take several trips. He used heavy black duffels that Gary had rolled up in the Bronco. He was covered in mud and there was no way not to get it all over Gary's seat. He'd get over it. He folded down the second-row seats to make more cargo room for the gold. He parked it closer to the Airbnb that where it was prior and under the biggest streetlight. He texted Possum and scaled the rear wall of the Airbnb. The bags were insanely heavy, so they needed to use leverage to get them over the wall. Possum quickly put together a simple pulley system using three heavy duty carabiners and some nylon cord. Once secure to the top of the wall, Rick scaled it again and Possum used the pulley system to get the bags over the wall. They placed them inside the back bedroom closet and Rick threw his muddy clothes in the washing machine and climbed into the shower. He was back in his bedroom at 11:54 p.m. He beat his goal of midnight by six minutes.

CHAPTER 16

Rick phone rang at 6:00am. He felt like he had just gone to sleep. It was Gary.

"Hey Rick, get me out of here."

"Oh my God man, you're alive?"

"Duh. I'm so freaking sore. When the barge blew, everything went black. Hang on the doctor just walked in."

Gary covered the headset with his palm and Rick could hear mumbling, then Gary cussed. He got back on.

"They don't want me to leave yet. They want me to stay one more day. I'm going stir crazy here."

"Can I speak to the doctor?" asked Rick.

"Hang on."

"Hello?"

"Hi Doctor, I'm Rick Waters, Gary's emergency contact.

Do you expect he will be released tomorrow? He said he would but I wanna hear it from the horse's mouth."

"I understand Mr. Waters. I can't say with hundred percent accuracy that he can leave tomorrow but I'd say there's a very good chance. He doesn't appear to have any brain injuries and all his cognitive responses seem normal. We want to run a HRNB on him tomorrow and if he does well on that we can release him."

"HRNB?" asked Rick.

"Oh sorry, HRNB is short for Halstead-Reitan Neuropsychological Battery test, which is a comprehensive suite comprising eight psychological tests designed to assess brain and nervous system function, as well as to evaluate the localization and lateralization of brain injuries. The test battery includes the Wechsler Intelligence Scale, Aphasia Screening Test, Trail Making Tests, and Halstead Category Tests—each of which consists of seven subtests. Anyway, it's the gold standard of brain injury tests. If he does well, he's gonna be good to go."

"Thank you doctor. Can we visit him?"

"When were you planning?"

"Sometime tomorrow."

"If you come after three o'clock tomorrow, he should be back in his room."

"Sounds good. We'll try and be there sometime after three. Can you put Gary back on?"

"Sure."

"Hey man, we are gonna come by tomorrow for a visit and possibly take you home if it all works out. Sound good?"

"What about the mission?" asked Gary.

"Dude, too much has gone down to discuss over a call. We'll all catch up tomorrow, okay?"

"Alright, see ya manana."

Rick was starting to feel better about things and kicked back his feet on the lounge chair in the back yard by the pool. Jules was reading a magazine beside him when Rick's phone rang. It was Carson.

"Rick, get out now! There's a million-dollar bounty for your head from the Alvarez cartel."

Suddenly gunfire erupted towards the front of the rental house. Machine guns were blazing and everyone took cover.

Rick hung up on Carson and grabbed Jules.

"Let's go!" he yelled.

The crew came scurrying out of the great room as bullets ripped through the windows and drywall. Rick grabbed his go bag and pulled out his .45 and tossed a shotgun to Possum. Clay was already carrying and began to return fire in the hallway. Two men kicked the front door open, and Clay could see one of the guards dead on the porch. He unloaded his Glock on the guy in the doorway and he fell backwards. Bullets continued to fly into the Airbnb as machine guns on full auto blasted the rental house. They were outnumbered and outgunned. Rick grabbed his other .45, and put two full clips in.

"Go, go, go to Gary's Bronco, I'll cover you. Meet me in the lobby of the Casa Marina. Go now!" shouted Rick as he tossed Clay the keys.

Rick fired both pistols out of the front door as fast as he could pull the trigger. He reloaded and continued to fire. Possum scaled the wall first and scanned the area for any gunmen. Clay helped Jules and P-Roy over the wall, then climbed over himself. They ran towards Gary's Bronco. Possum fired it up and they peeled out down Southern Street towards the Casa. He slammed on the brakes and gave the parking attendant twenty bucks.

"Keep it running."

They all piled out of the Bronco and into the Casa Marina lobby. They brought attention to themselves and were all out of breath. After a few minutes people ignored them. P-Roy and Possum took Jules to a seating area and Clay kept a lookout of the main entrance with his Glock hidden under his shirt. A few minutes later Rick came running up completely winded. He bent over trying to catch his breath and waved at Clay for them all to come out. He hopped in the driver's seat with Possum riding shotgun. Jules and Clay climbed in back.

"What are we gonna do?" asked Jules.

"We're gonna get the hell out of here. If they can't protect us, then we'll protect ourselves."

Rick raced to the Key West airport.

"Clay, get the jet ready, I'll be back as fast as I possibly can."

Jules pleaded with him to stay but Rick knew that they were in danger. So was Johnie. He had to get him out of the Lower Keys Medical Center and fast. Gary would be next. Rick parked the Bronco and calmly walked into the small hospital on College Road. He had no intention of waiting for Johnie to be released. He had to get him out without them knowing.

He asked for Johnie's room and search the hallways for a janitorial closet. He spotted it and when no one was looking put on a pair of oversized coveralls and a baseball cap, grabbed an extra pair of coveralls and a pushed a mop and bucket out of the doorway into the hall. He rolled it towards Johnie's room with the coveralls tucked into the zippered part of his own, making him look like he had a huge beer gut. When he got to Johnie's room, he looked around and strolled in.

"Rick?" asked Johnie.

"Here put this on. I'll explain later."

Johnie changed into the coveralls and Rick put a bunch of pillows under Johnie's hospital bed covers to resemble a body and then peered out into the hallway. He pushed the mop and bucket towards the back of the hospital as Johnie walked beside him, keeping his eyes down. Once they were out of the back door, Johnie dove into the back seat as Rick drove off. They made a beeline for the Airbnb.

"How's your strength Johnie?"

"I'm solid Rick. What's going on?"

"You'll see, climb up here."

Johnie crawled into the front seat and when they got a block from the Airbnb, they parked and snuck around the house beside the one they rented. Rick peered at the house they had just fled from and there seemed to be no activity.

"Follow me," Rick said to Johnie.

He scaled the wall after making sure everyone had gone. He could hear sirens in the distance and knew there wasn't much time. They ran in and he and Johnie pulled the black duffels towards what was left of the front door. There were so many bullet holes in the walls that it exposed the frame of the house. Rick leaned out of the front door and looked down at the two men who were meant to protect them. They were both so young. It was obvious they were dead from the amount of blood that was pooled up around them. There was nothing Rick could do to help them. Using all their strength they dragged the bags to the street and Rick ran down and pulled up next to the bags. Then he and Johnie lifted them into the back cargo space of the Bronco and Rick smoked the tires bound for the airport. He passed several Sheriff patrol units going the opposite way towards the Airbnb they had just left.

Rick pulled up next to Gary's jet and they all loaded the gold on board as Johnie parked the Bronco. Clay hid the gold in the false floor Gary had installed when he had the plane built. Rick put one bar in his backpack. Within ten minutes the jet lifted off the tarmac bound for Miami.

Rick's phone rang again. It was Carson.

"Rick where are you?"

"I'm on Gary's jet. We are going to get him."

"Rick some men went into the Lower Keys Medical Center and shot up the place. Five are dead and three wounded. They were going for Johnie."

"Damn! Johnie's with me. Five dead. That's horrible. I'm so furious. Can you get Gary to safety before we arrive?"

"Listen. I'll have some men get Gary. Text me when you land in Miami. Wait. Land at Fort Lauderdale Executive Airport instead. We are putting you all under protective custody. I'm bringing in the Secret Service. We have a safe house for you. I'll take care of Gary for you personally along with my men."

Clay adjusted his flight pattern for Ft Lauderdale and had to circle a few times to get clearance. When they landed there were five matching black Ford Tahoe's sitting on the Tarmac. As soon as the doors were opened, the secret service pulled up and rushed Rick and the crew into one of the Tahoe's. They rode in a side-by-side formation and changed positions several times. By the time they left the airport, Rick and the crew were in the third Tahoe.

"Are these windows bullet proof?" asked Rick.

"I'm not at liberty to say sir, you are in our protection

now. Turn on your phones if they aren't already on and pass them to me."

They all did as they were told the agent placed them in a black baggy. One of the SUV's pulled alongside and he passed the baggy to the driver. They immediately peeled away from the group and disappeared down some side roads. Rick knew exactly what they were doing. If one of their phones had a tracer on it the men from the cartel would follow the wrong SUV. They drove for several miles then turned onto US-1 and into the New River Tunnel. The SUV behind Rick and the crew stopped sideways and the one in front sped along and did the same. The driver stopped and they were all got out and moved into a white soccer mom's van going the opposed direction. It also had two cars with it. An older model lime green Ford Taurus and a blue Chevy Silverado 4x4. All three cars looked like civilian cars. Once they were inside the van, all three vehicles proceeded out of the tunnel with all the black SUV's heading the opposite way. That move impressed Rick. Changing cars is something bank robbers did. Apparently, the secret service learned a thing or two about get away drivers. They turned onto I-595 heading west and merged only Alligator Alley. Once they were on the straight away on I-75, the drive floored it and Rick looked over at the speedometer. They were doing over a hundred and fifteen.

"Holy shit, what's in the minivan?"

"I'm not at liber..."

"Liberty to say, I get it. I get it," interrupted Rick.

The driver gave Rick a quick grin in the rear-view mirror. Suddenly the van came to a quick stop and they turned into what looked like an overgrown road that ended at a vine covered fence just over the canal. Just as they were about to smash into the fence, it laid down flat and all three vehicles drove over it. Rick looked behind them and the fence popped right back into place.

Amazing! thought Rick.

They drove down the grass path that didn't resemble a road at all and soon under a canopy woven from palm fronds in between tall cypress trees. All three vehicles parked under the canopy surrounded my gumbo-limbo trees, mangroves, and bromeliads. From the air, it would look just like a patch of grass mounds. The driver let them out and led them to a steel door that opened revealing a large lush great room with five bedrooms and a massive kitchen on the far left. It was a beautiful home posing as a safe house. If someone was to walk in there blindfolded, then step outside. they'd never believe it was real. On the wall was several framed photos of many presidents. There were no windows and Rick was pretty sure the walls were also made of steel and concrete. The lights they used were all made to mimic sunlight including four faux skylights in the ceiling that looked like blue sky above. They even had moving clouds. The agents showed them to their rooms. Rick slid his backpack under the bed.

"When is Gary getting here?"

"I'm not at liberty..."

"Listen, We aren't prisoners here and I need you to answer certain questions," demanded Rick.

The agent whispered something into a mic in his collar.

"Okay. He will be here in fifteen minutes. He has been sedated. Two agents went onto get him and he thought they were cartel. He fought before the agents could show him their badges. For their own safety he was sedated. He's in good hands now. That's all I can tell you."

"What was he sedated with."

"I'm not at liberty to say sir," said the agent.

Jesus!

Twenty minutes later two agents came in, pushing Gary in a wheelchair. His head was held in place by a Velcro strap. He was out cold. They placed him on a bed in one of the bedrooms and left as quickly as they had arrived. Rick stepped into his room, and he was snoring.

"When will he wake up?" Never mind, I know, you're not at liberty to say," said Rick shaking his head.

Rick and the crew checked on him several times over the next few hours. About three hours into his slumber, he began to stir. Jules was in the room and called the boys in. Rick pulled the gold bar out of his bag, put it in his back pocket and stepped into the room.

"May we have some privacy?"

"Yes sir, we'll be right outside."

Rick pulled the door closed as Gary began to come to. He slowly opened his eyes and seemed disoriented. He reached for his head like he had so many times before after a night of drinking too much.

"Damn, did I get date raped? My head is pounding."

"I'm not at liberty to say," said Rick with a grin as he placed the gold bar into Gary's hand.

He looked down at it unsure what it was at first, then his eyes grew wide.

"You found it?!"

"Yep, found it, lost it, and found it again," said Rick.

"Where is it now?"

"It's on the jet, sitting on the Tarmac at Fort Lauderdale Executive Airport."

"Well, have Clay fly it out of there."

"That would be a problem since Clay is right here."

Clay leaned forward as Gary squinted to make out his face.

"Hi Boss!"

"Hey Clay. Hey everyone. Wow. You're all here, I see now. Is it my birthday?"

"Do you have amnesia?" asked Jules.

"Naw, I'm just messing with y'all,"

"I am a little confused though. The last thing I remember was these two guys rushing into my room right after I took some test the doctor set up for me. I was just coming out of the bathroom, and they reached for me. I slammed one hard and then everything went black. They looked like cartel guys."

"They were secret service. You never gave them time to show their ID's. So, I guess they either tazed you, drugged you or both."

"Secret service? What the hell? From the way my head feels, I was drugged. Probably the date rape drug, GHB."

"You've been out of the loop. Let me get you up to speed. Ready for a story?" asked Rick.

"Let's hear it," said Gary as he puffed up his pillow.

Rick told Gary about everything he had missed when he was knocked unconscious from the explosion on the barge. At the end of Rick's story Gary looked around as if he was missing someone.

"Where's Sebastian?"

"We think he's in Greece. I found some evidence he took a nonstop to Athens. I think he got spooked. He pretty much knows everyone and everything that goes down in Key West. Someone probably gave him the heads up that he was in danger from the cartel, and he high tailed it. He's smart enough not to make contact until this is all over," said Rick.

"What's the plan?" asked Gary.

"I wish I knew. These guys are sworn to secrecy, and you can barely get any info from them. I have no idea where our phones are. The whole thing makes me nervous. Juan and I are the main people to testify against Alvarez. I imagine the trial is on the fast track. Unfortunately, some of the men in the cartel are loyal to Alvarez. I don't even know if Juan is still alive. Most of his men were killed when they tried to double-cross us on the ship."

Suddenly there was a knock on the door.

"Yes?"

"Mr. Waters, you need to come with me. Everyone else will stay here."

"Where are we going? Never mind, I know your answer."

They escorted Rick to the one of the black SUV's that had now been parked under the hidden canopy. They drove fast down I-75 east towards Ft Lauderdale. Soon they were on the 15th avenue and pulled onto the Army Reserve Base. Rick was escorted to a Chinook helicopter and within minutes they took off southbound. Before long they had crossed over the Florida Keys and continued straight south. Rick could see mountains in the distance.

Cuba? he thought.

The chopper sat down and several military guys escorted Rick into a building. As he walked into a room the door behind him was closed. There was a table and two chairs. A door in the back of the room opened and in walked Carson.

"Sorry about all the cloak and dagger," said Carson as he reached out to shake Ricks hand.

"No kidding. I feel like I've been tossed around in a washing machine. What's going on?"

"Do you know where are?"

"Guantanamo Bay?"

"Good guess. You're in an area known as Guantánamo's Expeditionary Legal Complex. This building was built after 911 to try the men responsible for that atrocity. It's a courthouse inside of a base. We are trying Alvarez here."

"When?" asked Rick,

"Tomorrow. We are just waiting for Juan Esteban. He was wounded. Well, twice. Once when he was shot outside of your ship and then some men tried to take him out so he couldn't testify. They can't get to us here. Alvarez will be tried here and never see the light of day after this. He'll never leave this island."

"And Juan?"

"He doesn't know it yet but he will be given immunity."

"Immunity? What the fuck? He tried to kill me. Kill us!"

"Look Rick. Immunity may sound good but once the trial is over, he will be deported back to Colombia. That's essentially a death sentence. Those men loyal to Alvarez will take him out. We are preparing an invasion of Alvarez's homes, labs and poppy fields in joint cooperation with the Colombian authorities. Come this time next week, the only thing left of Alvarez's operation will be ashes."

"Karma, instant karma," said Rick.

CHAPTER 17

The sound of tocororo birds singing their song of freedom awakened Rick from his slumber. Ironic, he thought, considering in a few hours Alvarez would most likely lose his freedom for the rest of his natural life in the trial. Rick stumbled to the mess hall and ate breakfast with all the other soldiers on that Godforsaken base. He got the feeling no one really wanted to be there. For only a few yards away behind the ten-foot fence topped with razor wire were many of the 911 conspirators and perps. Hatred seemed to fill the air.

Rick showered after breakfast and got dressed in the same clothes they brought him in. It's all he had to wear. He was escorted to the courthouse by two soldiers. The dingy cavern-like courthouse was a dimly lit and damp underground facility located within Guantanamo Bay Naval Base.

The entrance to the courthouse was inconspicuous weathered wooden door leading down a narrow, winding staircase. Once inside, the ambiance was unsettling with flickering overhead lights casting eerie shadows on the rough-hewn walls. The air was musty and heavy, carrying a distinct smell of dampness and mildew. The ceiling was low, giving the impression of being enclosed and confined.

The courtroom itself was small and claustrophobic, with worn wooden benches and a few uncomfortable chairs for the legal counsel. The judge's bench was elevated, but the surroundings lack the grandeur and prestige usually associated with conventional courthouses. The walls had peeling paint, and lacked proper ventilation that made the atmosphere stifling. Dim, dusty windows allow only a faint glimmer of light to filter through, further contributing to the gloomy and ominous atmosphere.

"All Rise, the honorable Judge Advocate General's Corps Harold Bostwick presiding," said the bailiff.

"Mr. Diego Alvarez, you stand before this court with seventy-seven counts of drug trafficking, fifty-two counts of money laundering and nine counts of racketeering. How do you plead?" asked the judge.

"I plead not guilty," said Alvarez.

He was clad in an orange jump suit and both his hands and feet were in shackles. He failed to conceal the aura of menace he exuded, when strode into the courtroom with his head held high. His eyes locking with the judge's as he asserted his innocence. At his side an appointed defense attorney named Vincent Shaw took the stage, but it quickly became apparent that Shaw was out of his depth. Nervous and unsteady, his arguments were feeble, and failed to match the prosecution's piercing accusations.

The prosecution presented its first witness, Rick Waters, a man whose soul bore the scars of what he'd been through. As he took the stand he took a deep breath, aware of the risk he was taking by testifying against the cartel kingpin. Waters recounted tales of the sunken dC-3 filled with drug making laboratory equipment, clandestine phone meetings, and brutal violence; all intricately tied to Diego Alvarez. The courtroom listened in silence, captivated by the raw details that came to light.

Next, Juan Esteban, Alvarez's former underboss stepped into the witness box, his face obscured by the shadows of his past life. A man torn between loyalty and self-preservation; Esteban hesitated before revealing the darkest secrets of the cartel. With a trembling voice, he recounted chilling accounts of Alvarez's direct involvement in the illegal operations—cementing the case against him.

Throughout the trial Alvarez maintained his composure, revealing only a hint of fury beneath his controlled exterior. But the relentless waves of damning evidence crashed against his defense like a hurricane upon a frail vessel.

In the climax of the trial, the defense attorney's final attempt to undermine the prosecution's case fell flat. He failed to dismantle the credibility of the key witnesses or cast doubt upon their motives. The room hung in an eerie silence as the judge deliberated the fate of the cartel boss.

The verdict came down like a sledgehammer, crushing any hope of freedom for Diego Alvarez. Guilty on all counts. The judge's words reverberated throughout the courtroom; the weight of the sentence causing Alvarez to falter for the first time. Life in prison without the chance of parole - a sentence that echoed with finality, drowning the once powerful crime lord in a sea of despair.

As the gavel struck, sealing Alvarez's fate, the courtroom lawyers put away papers and closed briefcases in such a nonchalant way, it was as if they already knew what the verdict would be before any of them entered the courtroom, a kangaroo court. Shadows of the cartel still loomed, but justice had prevailed and society could breathe a collective sigh of relief, knowing that Diego Alvarez would forever be confined behind the bars he once thought he was untouchable by. The entire trial lasted less than three hours and it felt like a slam dunk for the prosecution.

In Guantanamo you are guilty until proven innocent, or, more appropriately, always guilty regardless, thought Rick.

Within an hour Rick was back on board the Military chopper bound for Florida. Within a few hours Rick was back in Ft Lauderdale and soon back in the safe house. He was certain that after that conviction, they'd be safe to leave on their own soon. He was wrong. The Feds underestimated the loyalty of some of Alvarez's men. Once word got out that Alvarez was found guilty a new bounty of five million dollars had been placed on Ricks head.

"We are moving to another location. We have intel that this place may have been revealed to the cartel," said the agent in charge.

"Now wait a damn minute. This place has been a safe house for many a dignitary I'm sure over the years, and you're telling me that now we are in danger here. We have a mole! I felt it before and now I know. Someone on the inside is feeding the cartel intel about us. We are sitting ducks. I have one more question. Are we under arrest or being forced to stay in this hole? I also demand that you give us our phones back. Don't worry, I won't put the batteries in until we are far away from here."

"Mr. Waters, we feel it's in your best interest to have the help of the secret service. Where else would you be safer?" asked the agent.

"I'm not at liberty to say. Give us a car. Now!"

The agent stepped away and came back a few minutes later with a set of keys and some paperwork for Rick to sign.

"Rental agreement?" asked Rick with a chuckle.

"No sir, it's a requisition form, standard procedure."

"Jesus, can't you guys tell when I'm joking? Always so serious. We'll be ready to go in a few minutes."

Rick went into the master bedroom and called the crew in with him. They all gathered round as he whispered.

"We must get away from these guys. Someone is feeding the cartel info on our whereabouts. We are safer away from them. They always seem to be one step ahead of us. Is the jet ready Clay?"

"Yes, it was refueled and it's just sitting there. Where are we going?"

"File a flight plan to Destin. I'll tell you where when we are in the air."

"Gotcha."

They all filed out of the bedroom and into the white minivan. Rick would've preferred the SUV but then again, the engine in this thing was awe inspiring. He knew he would be followed by them, so he didn't even try to outrun them. They had every intention of keeping their eyes on them. Once they arrived at the private airport, Clay prepared the jet and filed a flight plan. They were wheels up shortly after they arrived. Rick whispered in Clays ear a new destination then went back to the main cabin.

"Listen ya'll, everyone including the cartel thinks we are bound for Destin. It would only be a matter of time until they make a run at us. I had a long meeting with Carson, and he is forwarding me the names of the top five cartel underbosses and their muscle. They will be coming for us. The one thing they would never suspect is us going for them. What do you say?" asked Rick.

"We're going to Colombia?" asked Possum.

"Yep, unless anyone wants off, we, can make a stop."

Rick was about to tell Jules that she would be holed up in the penthouse suite of Four Seasons Bogota, when he saw her putting on her tactile gear and matching .45's. He knew she would not be sitting this one out and there was no way of talking her out of it. Besides they needed her. She spoke the perfect dialect of Spanish. She would be their interpreter and liaison.

"So, what's the plan Rick?" asked Gary.

"I know that they are turning over Juan to the Colombian authorities. He was given immunity for his testimony against Alvarez. The Colombians are so corrupt, they will release him immediately. It's a death sentence for him. They will try to ambush him the first chance they get, and we need to ambush their ambush. Carson will be sending me over photos. He said the CIA is planning a mission to take out the cartel but there's so much bureaucracy that it could take months. We don't have months. Clay how's your chopper course going. You ready to put it to the test?"

"I've never solved before."

"You won't be solo; Possum and I will be with you." said Rick with a wink.

"Possum, remember that MOAB you said you've always wanted to build?" asked Rick.

"Yeah? Why?"

"What do you need to build it?"

Possum grabbed a notebook and started writing down items.

1000 lbs of RDX (Cyclotrimethylene trinitramine)

100 sticks of TNT

400 lbs of Powdered aluminum

Firing pin or phone detonator

"How are we delivering this device? I need to know what kind of fuse to light, so to speak."

"We are gonna drive it right inside their compound in one of their own vehicles," replied Rick.

"Gary and I can go with Jules and secure the explosive parts. She can do the talking and we can protect her. Where do we buy this stuff?"

"We don't. We steal it," said Rick.

"Are you nuts? From whom?"

"Not whom exactly, but where. From the air force base in Malambo. We are landing in Barranquilla, a short drive there. They keep all unspent ordinances there that are seized. You may not be able to build an actual MOAB but a mini 'Mother Of All Bombs' will do."

The plane touched down in Barranquilla and Jules secure them two rental cars. Both were matching Range Rovers. Rick, Clay and Johnie took one; and Jules, Possum and Gary took the other. One SUV would hunting down explosive parts and the other would be hunting down drug kingpins.

Rick loaded the SUV with enough firepower to start a war and headed towards a known mansion of Alvarez. Three of the top men had taken over the home in Soledad. They once were street soldiers for Alvarez but now they were drunk on power. This would be a sniper operation.

Once near the outskirts of the plush mansion, Rick found a treelined area with a good view of the side terrace where meetings often occurred—according to intel from Carson. They often sat out by that pool, drank expensive cocktails, and made plans as if they were kings of the world. Rick forwarded the photos of the men to each of their phones. All they had to do was wait. As happy-hour time approached, Rick could see activity on the pool deck. Women were setting out trays of snack and bottles for their bosses. They all studied the deck through the scopes of their Barrett Mk22 sniper rifles.

"There's one. The guy in the brown Versace polo shirt is mine. That's Carlos Lopez. Johnie, you take out Matias Menendez, he's the guy who just sat down in red button-down. There's still one more. His name is Fernando Lozano. He's yours Clay. Can you do this? I know this isn't your normal job description and killing someone if it's the first time may be hard. I gave you Fernando because he is one of the most ruthless killers Alvarez has. He is suspected of killing an entire family in Cartagena. He even stomped a baby to death."

"I got this. That makes me sick," replied Clay.

"Okay, according to his last known photo he has one side of his head shaved and he wears a ton of jewelry. He won't be hard to spot if he's there."

Just as Rick finished his sentence the gawdy dressed Lozano came strolling out of the main house with two bikini clad women his arms. He sent them away once he sat at the main table with the other two men.

"We must fire together. On my count. Also, double tap to make sure they are gone."

They both nodded.

"Give me a sign when you have your target."

"Go," said Johnie.

"I got him," said Clay.

"On three. One two three!"

Pew, Pew!

Two of the men fell backwards and one slumped over his seat. They continued to watch through the scopes as the hired help came running out. It was clear by the looks on their faces and the way they scrambled to get out of the line of fire that the men were dead. They watched their lifeless bodies for a few more seconds then loaded up the guns as Rick drove off.

"Three down, a dozen to go!" said Rick.

Rick was trying to take out any possible successors to the Alvarez cartel and end it once and for all. They had wreaked too much havoc and death on the people of Colombia and the US. They had to go.

Possum pulled the SUV behind the Restaurante Bar Joselo de Colombia, a poplar bar for military men near the base. Jules changed into a seductive dress and strolled into the bar. She sized up two of the guys that would fit the bill and coaxed them outside. They followed her around back like puppy dogs and once they were out of sight, Gary and Possum used Pulse subcompact stun guns and fired simultaneously at the unsuspecting flyboys. Once they were subdued, Possum injected them with a healthy dose of Brexanolone, one of the many go-to's in his medical kit. Besides being a critical thinker, Possum had become a critical planner as well. It would cause no lasting effects on the men but should put them down for a couple of hours. They dragged them behind some trees and removed their uniforms and ID and changed into them. Possum leaned them against the trees and propped their heads down so their faces couldn't be clear and snapped a couple of pics with his iPhone.

Once they arrived at the base, they escorted Jules inside.

"We need to take this woman in for questioning. She is under suspicion of drugging and stealing from some of the men on the base here. Two of them are now in hospital and were found drugged near the Lobo Cocktail bar."

Possum showed them the photo of the flyboys he took. The Lobo Cocktail Bar was on the other side of town but also known to be frequented by the Airforce guys on their off time. The MP's escorted Jules to a holding area, as Possum and Gary tagged along.

"I will let the Air Base Commander know," said the MP.

"I've already spoken with him. He's expecting us. That'll be all. We'll take it from here."

As soon as the men went back to their posts, Possum went into action. He walked with a determination and confidence that he belonged there and was not questioned by anyone of any rank. Once he got access to the munitions building, he loaded a cargo truck with everything he needed and forged the documents that looked like he'd be disposing of spent ordinances. He texted Gary and they slipped around the back of the M939 series 5-ton 6×6 truck and climbed under some camo canvass. Once outside the gate, he drove towards the rented SUV. Gary climbed out and followed them. They ditched the big truck in the rainforest and transferred the cargo to the Range Rover just outside of town. Now they needed to get it to the main compound in Bogota. They headed back to the airport and reported to Rick who was already on his way.

They loaded the bomb making material in the plane and Clay had it refueled. They took off for Bogota. It was time for part two of the operation. Rick jokingly named it *The Juan Who Got Away*. Word on the street was that whoever took out Juan would be named the new Narco. All the higher up guys were vying for that spot, and it would be their best chance to get them all together. They landed in Bogota just after dark and everyone except Possum and Clay took off for the Four Seasons. They would stay with the jet as Possum built the explosive device.

Carson texted Rick.

> Esteban will be arriving at Bogota International at 08:00 and transport-
> ed to the Colombia National Police Headquarters Orchestra. The hit will
> most likely occur after the left turn on Av. Boyacá and Sur / Calz Later-
> al. Rick pulled out his MacBook and opened Google Earth and wrote
> down the most likely perimeter for the hit on Juan Esteban. They just
> needed to expand that perimeter and when the shooting begins, they
> will know their targets. It would take everyone on the team.

RICK TEXTED Possum and keyed him in. He replied that they both be back at the hotel by 6:00am. That would give them time to get armed and into position. Jules would be with Rick and be his support for the Barrett. They each teamed up with the long rifles as a duo. Possum and Clay, Gary and Johnie. P-Roy would man the comms and be speaking directly to Carson and relay any route changes to Rick and the team.

THE STREETS WERE ALREADY busy with locals headed to work and people shopping. Rick knew the cartel didn't care about collateral damage, but he did. The less innocent lives that could be spared the better. It was go-time.

CHAPTER 18

The C-130 touched down at 7:51am. Its cargo was but one thing, Juan Esteban. Once on the tarmac, the Colombian authorities loaded him into the back of an armored escort van and left the airport along with three matching other vans and some federal police in Jeeps with gun turrets. They would be slaughtered by the cartel. As the vans proceeded down Av. El Dorado towards the left turn to the police headquarters, Rick scanned the area in front of him with his scope as Jules did the same with binoculars.

"Four o'clock, jogging suit, just stepped out of that Cadillac." said Jules.

"I got him. Also, six o'clock, dark hair, briefcase," replied Rick.

"I see him."

Rick steadied his Barrett. The silencers Johnie and

Possum had designed were some of the quietest ones Rick had ever used. As bad as he wanted to shoot, he had to wait until they fired first. Even though they had spotted two of them already, they hoped the other guys on the team had seen their targets as well. There had to be at least a dozen or so to deal with. He was waiting the signal from P-Roy. Sweat dripped own Rick's forehead as he gripped the gun tighter.

> *They are turning now.*

Texted P-Roy to Rick, Gary and Possum.

Rick looked up the road and saw the white vans following one of the turret mounted Jeeps. It was just too damn obvious. As they got closer, Rick keyed in on the man with the briefcase. He opened it and pulled out two Mac10's. They had no silencers. All hell was about to break loose on the streets of Colombia. As the Jeep approached Rick could see the man in the jogging suit taking aim at the gunman on top of the Jeep.

Rick could wait any longer. He aimed for his chest, squinted, and slowly pulled the trigger. It looked like slow motion as the man's chest caved in and he slumped over falling backwards behind a bush. Before he hit the ground gunfire erupted from all directions towards the vans. Within seconds they were riddled with bullet holes. Rick took out the second guy with the briefcase. His Mac-10's still firing as they fell to the ground. With the flash of every gun towards the van, Rick and the gang found their targets. In less than two minutes, all guns had ceased fire. The front two vans had crashed off to the side of the road. The third one was disabled, and Rick could see the doors open as two guards pulled Esteban out to get him to safety.

One to go.

Rick was careful and patient to get a shot. He couldn't let Esteban live. He'd finish what the cartel started with the slow squeeze of the trigger. He had him in his sights and they paused for a split second at the end of the van. Rick took his shot. Direct to the head of Esteban. Blood splattered across the side of the van and the men carrying him ducked for cover. His limp body lay in a pool of blood on the dirty street he once planned to hold court over.

Jules jogged down the hill and climbed in the Cadillac that was still running near the first man Rick took out. She dragged the man into the backseat and he slumped over. She drove straight for the airport. Rick hopped in the Range Rover and they all rendezvoused by the jet. The private area Clay parked the Jet was on the far east side of the international airport and had lax security. No one even asked them for ID when they parked beside the jet to load the bomb into the Cadillac. Once the bomb was placed inside the trunk, Rick drove with Possum riding shotgun and Johnie in the back seat propping up the dead man.

Clay secured a helicopter and got prepared for his first ever solo flight. He felt confident he could do it. He'd taken off and landed many times with his instructor back in Destin, but this flight would be his final test. He took off and set his pattern for the main drug lab of the former boss, Diego Alvarez. Since it was the Sabbath, there would be very few people working the lab. As ruthless and destructive as Alvarez was, he was also Catholic; and as hypocritical as it was, he believed Sundays were a day for rest and worship. Only a skeleton crew of armed guards were left at the compound. There would be an inevitable gunfight once they realized what was going down.

Rick slowly approached the main gate of the drug compound; his hat was pulled down and he was wearing black out shades, as was Possum. Johnie lay in the backseat propping up the dead gunman like some Spanish version of *Weekend at Bernie's*. As they approached the gate, Rick lowered the back window and Johnie did his magic hand trickery to make him wave and nod. They drove right inside and parked by the large building.

Rick texted Clay the signal. Possum set the timer for three minutes and they climbed out of the Cadillac, guns blazing. Rick took out two guards quickly, as bullets flew into the Cadillac's front window sending glass fragments flying. They ran towards the main gate blasting their fully automatic guns in all directions. As they ran a bullet grazed Johnie's right arm and which caused him to drop his weapon. Rick grabbed it and tossed it back to him as he rolled to the right, opening fire on two more guards running towards them. Possum lead the way through the gate and they ran as fast as they could as bullets pinged all around them kicking up dust. They turned the corner where the road split. They were out of bullet range but not out of danger.

"One minute Rick!"

Clay sat the chopper down in an open field about a hundred yards from the compound. They all leapt inside as he lifted off. He accelerated towards the mountain keeping close to the treetops. The mini-MOAB had a three-hundred-yard blast zone and the concussion could be strong enough to blow them out of the sky. The chopper scrapped the leaves of the tree as it just cleared the mountain and began its descent to the other side.

"Three, two, one," counted Possum.

Nothing.

"What happened?" asked Rick.

"I don't know, maybe one of the bullets damaged the timer."

"What can we do?"

"We have to manually detonate it," said Possum.

"You mean shoot it?"

"I guess. Can you hit the trunk with the Barrett?"

"I can try. Get me over the top. There aren't many guards

left and they all have submachine guns. We'll be out of their range at fifteen hundred yards."

Clay maneuvered the chopper directly above the compound. A few guards were firing in the air at the chopper, but it was futile. It was like trying to hit a dove with a sling shot. Rick leaned against the side of the door and took aim at the Cadillac's trunk. He held his breath and fired. A cloud of dust kicked up beside the rear tire. He missed. He pulled off the magazine and there were only two rounds of 7.62mm left. He had two chances. They were out of ammo for that gun and there was no other gun they had that could do it from that range. Getting closer would mean being killed by the blast themselves.

Rick took aim again.

Pew.

The edge of the trunk bent as the bullet slammed into it.

Closer, thought Rick.

Rick pulled the bolt action one more time and loaded the last bullet into the chamber. He aimed and squeezed the trigger.

Smash!

The rear window shattered. He missed again.

"Fuck it. Take us down at an angle," said Possum as he wrapped electrical tape around three sticks of dynamite.

"Cover me."

Rick and Gary leaned out of the chopper as Possum lit the short fuse. They began unloading magazines on the guards still alive, as the chopper dove towards the Cadillac. Possum laid down on the floor with his head hanging out of the Chopper and reached back and flung the dynamite towards the Cadillac. It hit the roof and bounced then fell into the back seat.

"Pull up, pull up,"

With full throttle Clay lifted the chopper straight up. They had to get out of the blast zone fast.

Kaboom! Boom, boom!

The dynamite set off the mini-MOAB and a mushroom cloud lifted directly below them. The chopper began to shake and vibrate violently as the cloud overtook them. The sky went black, and Clay lost control of the chopper and it began to spin.

"We're going down!" yelled Clay.

Clay hit the collective pitch lever and held the stick tight trying to stop the spin. As the chopper began to fall the main engine died from all the dust particles from the explosion. The chopper was falling at a high rate of speed and just before they reached the treetops, Clay flared the rotors, causing autorotation and they slowed down and slammed into the trees ripping the blades off the chopper and breaking tree limbs, and it fell towards the ground. About twenty feet from the ground, the chopper came to a sudden stop as the tail got hung in the tree. They all flew forward, and Possum almost went through the front glass.

"It everyone alright?" asked Rick breathlessly.

Possum's forehead was bleeding and Johnie dislocated his shoulder. Rick was uninjured and he helped Clay get his seat belt loose.

"We have to get out before this thing falls! The tank is nearly full." yelled Clay.

Possum ripped the side door open and climbed onto the tree, followed by Clay. Rick tried to help Johnie down but couldn't climb down with his shoulder injury.

"Throw down the cargo net!" yelled Clay.

Rick unbuckled the net that kept the luggage in the rear and tossed it down to Clay. He then climbed down. The three of them held out the cargo net.

"You have to jump Johnie!" yelled Possum.

"I'm scared."

Smoke was billowing out of the engine as he looked down.

"That thing might blow while you're up there. Come on man. You can do it," holler Rick.

Johnie maneuver himself to the door, closed his eyes and jumped. He slammed into the cargo net and yelled from the pain in his shoulder.

"Let's go!"

They all ran as flames began to appear and rise up to the tail.

Boom!

The helicopter exploded, sending fragments into the trees. They all dove for cover and weren't hit. There was a collective silence and only fast breathing as they stood up and looked back towards the flames in the trees.

"I hope you took out insurance," said Rick humorously as he patted Clay on the shoulder.

He ripped off his shirt and made a sling for Johnie. The bullet from the gun battle had barely nicked his arm and the cut had already stopped bleeding.

"We need a lift!"

Possum looked at his iPhone and got the GPS coordinates of where they were. He texted it to P-Roy.

> *Tell Jules, we are all okay. Mission complete. Come get us.*

P-Roy texted back a different GPS location and directions,

> *Open field, two clicks ESE. Blackhawk en route.*

"They're sending a rescue chopper for us. Follow me."

Rick led the way using his built in GPS in his phone, Johnie was lagging and in pain but kept up as best as he could. They all arrived in the woods beside the field as the chopper made its approach. Once on the ground, they bolted to the side door and climbed in.

"Welcome aboard. I'm First Lieutenant Randy Kent, US 75th Ranger Regiment. We're taking you to Tolemaida. The rest of your crew has already been transported there."

"Thank you, Lieutenant," said Rick as he shook his hand vigorously.

When they arrived on the tarmac at the base in Tolemaida, Jules and P-Roy were waiting to greet them. Another familiar face popped up as they landed. It was Carson. Jules ran to the chopper and threw her arms around Rick as he barely stepped down.

"Congratulations Rick. You did it."

"Did what?"

"Exactly, there will be no press about this, and I was never here."

What Rick and the Crew had done was singlehandedly take down one of the most ruthless cartels in Colombian history. The only press anyone in the US would see is that a rival cartel took down Alvarez's group. The war on drugs would continue but a big hole had been punched in the delivery of Fentanyl and many live would be save because of it. The US and any government authorities wouldn't acknowledge any responsibility for the action.

"Can I get a lift? Now that this is done, I'm, I mean we are meeting with the task force at Gary's fish camp. Forensics has some news we all want to hear.

After being debriefed they all were escorted back to El Dorado International airport in Bogota and released on their own recognizance by Gary's jet. Clay made a flight plan for Marcos Executive Airport, the closest airport to the Everglades. Rick reset Johnie's shoulder on the flight and his scream could be heard from thirty thousand feet. He would be sore, but he would heal. Possum would have little war scar on his forehead, but he would be fine as well.

Once they arrived at the airport, they all climbed into a rented van waiting for them, provided by the FBI. Carson drove. They were out of danger now. There was no one left in the cartel to take their revenge on Rick and the crew. They all felt a sense of relief when they got to the fish camp and were greeted by the caretaker. There was a huge area of crime tape around the explosion. Tables had been set up in the back yard with pieces of the lab and what was left of the burned money sitting on them marked as evidence.

"Forensics put a lot of work into this, and I guess it was kind of a waste of time since Alvarez was convicted, and Esteban is dead, but it did reveal something you might like to know," said Carson.

"Do tell," said Rick.

"Let's go inside where we can talk in comfort. These

damn mosquitos down here love me," said Carson as he was slapping them away.

They all gathered in the great room of Gary's stilt house and Carson laid out what they had discovered.

"Rick you were right about a mole. We've had suspicions of one of our own, for some time. He wasn't on my team directly but was one of the computer specialist agents working on logistics. We found out he had received several wire transfers from Colombia to his own personal account. They came from a shell company that Alvarez owned that was tied to his shipping business. When we confronted him about the payments he sang like a canary. He implicated someone else. Besides sending info directly to Esteban, he was also sending it to someone else. We weren't sure at first and didn't believe him, but DNA proved it.

"What DNA?" asked Rick.

"We took DNA from a finger we found in the swamp behind the house. We also found part of a burner phone and manage to salvage the sim card. Phone records revealed he was communicating to our guy on the inside."

"Who?!"

"The DNA is a perfect match for Sebastian Pappas. There were two moles. We checked the flight manifest for the flight number you gave us, and he never got on that plane to Greece. He flew that day, only in little pieces all over the Everglades."

"Dammit, I had high hopes for that kid."

"Greed will getcha every time," said Carson.

"Yeah, it will," agreed Rick.

"Well, I just need you to sign off on a few things and I'm out of here. This case or lack thereof is officially closed and I was never here. You can return the van whenever or one of our guys will. I'm going back with Jones, that guy down there who just finished bagging the evidence that we will dispose of for you."

"I like that plan, Carson. Thanks again for everything."

They shook hands and Carson rode off in an unmarked car. They all let out a sigh. It was over. It sort of felt anticlimactic at this point to Rick. He was saddened that Sebastian tried to steal the money and got himself killed.

"Well at least we got the gold. It's too bad Sebastian blew up all the cash. Carson said they only found a few burned up hondos," said Rick.

"Oh, I forgot to tell you," said Gary, as he rolled up the corner of the area rug.

He lifted open a trap door, pulled out a black duffel bag, unzipped it and kicked it over to Rick.

"Remember when I came here while you got Jules at the golf course?"

"Yeah,"

"Well, I started thinking about the mole and decided to move the money. I left a few stacks of Benjamin's just in case I was right. And I was. I got a hunch there were two moles and it had to be either P-Roy or Sebastian. No offense P-Roy," said Gary.

"None taken."

"Are you telling me you got all the money?"

"Yeah, there are five more duffle bags."

"You clever son of a bitch! How the hell are we even gonna clean this money?"

"There's a pretty good casino in Aruba. We can take the ship there and stroll in like high rollers. Cash in, play a little, then cash out. It's not too crazy far from the Panama Canal. I heard the fishing this time of year is insane in Cabo."

"Jules, you wanna get married in Mexico?" asked Rick.

THE END

Manufactured by Amazon.ca
Acheson, AB